18

Nicola

CW00406395

Topaz Butterfly

Alex B Taylor

Best Regards
Alex. B. Taylor

I wish to thank my son Scott and my daughter Sharon for the unending encouragement in the writing of this book. And also, my partner Isabella for her diligence and time spent proofreading the novel.

Calum could feel his eyes getting heavy and sore, could it be the fetid fumes that were coming from the flickering candle flames, or perhaps the worn out old wick in the oil lamp spiralling upwards to linger in the air, or was it just the tiredness that came from the constant peering at the intricate twists and curling of the positioning of the fine strands of gold and silver filigree inside the pendant which he had been toiling over for the past few days? But, nevertheless, he wasn't going to be distracted from finishing this fine piece.

It was getting late and, after a busy and hectic day, John Sinclair began cleaning the tools that he had been using, before tidying up the bench, which was now littered with fine pieces of gold and silver strands of wire. John was an artisan silversmith who was known throughout the city of Edinburgh for his expertise and craftsmanship. He was regarded in such high esteem that other fellows of the trade would come to him for advice, knowing that John was always glad to be of assistance. It was rumoured that even his Majesty, The Prince of Wales had, at some time, worn some of his designs at state occasions, such was his reputation.

John was a portly 48 year old man with a stooped posture, caused mainly from all the time spent hovered over a work-bench in the cramped confines of his workshop. But he was still very spry, his only affliction being his eyesight, which seemed to be getting weaker by the day, but he wasn't allowing this to deter him, as he derived great satisfaction from producing his works of art. As he approached the front door of the shop, he caught a glimpse of light coming from beneath the door of the small back room. Upon opening the door slightly, John was somewhat surprised to see his young nephew, Calum; still toiling away crouched over what appeared to be a gold pendant.

"Ah see yer still here son, it's ower late, ah thocht ye wid hae left afore noo, come alang hame wi' me an get tae yer bed."   The sound of John's voice broke the young man's concentration, startling him into dropping the fine strand of silver he was about to place into the pendant. "Ah'll be hame shortly faither, ah want tae feenish this piece, you carry on an' ah'll lock up." Giving a curt nod towards Calum, John smiled "Alright laddie. Goodnicht, ahn ah'll see ye the morn."

Closing the door and stepping into the cold wintry night, John was welcomed by a maelstrom of the snow and gale force winds which had begun earlier in the day and, within minutes, he was completely covered in a thick mantle of snow, giving him the appearance of a spectral apparition as he shuffled along blindly in a crouching position, with half-closed eyes, trying to fight against the onslaught of the wind, as it drove the snow unmercifully against his face. Suddenly, and without warning, the ferocity of the wind died off, leaving behind a comforting peacefulness that always seems to occur after a storm, and the cold grey wintry evening slowly diminished into the crepuscular twilight. The only sound to break the silence came from the crisp snow being trod underfoot by John, as he slowly walked home along the Royal Mile to where his house was situated. This was an affluent part of the city, occupied mostly by the professional bodies.

Over the years, John's business had flourished, to the point that he was in the position to purchase a grand house in this district, consisting of four large rooms and a few acres of land, which also had a gazebo that stood in a small clearing behind the house, where he would sit with Jean and while away the hours in the cool of the summer evenings. He had also purchased a small cottage beside the coast, to have the small comfort of retreating there for some complete rest and get some respite from his daily toil and to relax for a few days with Jean. Those days were a far cry from the present, as John found the streets deserted, because the snow was now falling faster and heavier and becoming deeper with every step he took.

Approaching his front door, John shook the snow from his wet coat and shivered, as he rubbed his hands up and down his arms in an attempt to warm his body from the chill. Once inside, he lit some candles and lamps before putting a light to the peat in the hearth. "This is no a nicht for man nor beast tae be oot," he thought to himself. As he removed his damp coat, he began pouring himself a small dram to take away the chills, before settling his weary body into his comfortable old chair. Coming home to an empty house was still foreign to him. It had been two lonely, long years since his wife Jean had died... his "Bonnie Jean," whom he had wed many years before. Closing his eyes and resting his head against the top of the chair, he began reminiscing, thinking back to the days when the sounds of laughter and happiness filled their home, as Jean would play all sorts of children's games with Calum. This was a small consolation, but it was all he had to keep her memory alive. He then let his thoughts stray to the day that Calum had come into their lives.

2

John's sister, Catriona, was married and heavily pregnant when her husband Ranald MacLean, who was part of the Jacobite rising for Prince Charles Edward Stuart, was killed at the battle of Culloden on April 16th 1746. When Catriona was informed of this tragic event, the shock was enough to put her into premature labour and, after two days, she gave birth to her son. The long excruciating labour pains of the pending birth of their baby, and the recent knowledge of her husband's death, seemed to be too much for her to bear, and sadly, Catriona appeared to give up the will to live and, closing her eyes, she succumbed.

The baby was now virtually an orphan, so John and Jean immediately took the child into their home to be raised by them. In a strange way, this was a blessing in disguise as, after 30 years of marriage, they had been unable to conceive a child. Now Jean quickly realized that she would have to hire a wet nurse from the village to wean the child, since he was only hours old and this was the only source of nourishment for him.

A few months later they had him baptised, naming him Calum and, within the year, young Calum grew stronger, so the need for the wet nurse was no longer required, as he was now graduating to eating solid food. Calum was the joy of their lives. While Jean taught him by schooling at home, John, weather permitting, would take his son fishing, or sometimes taking long walks through the woods showing the boy how wonderful nature could be, until it came to the stage the boy could name every tree and all the creatures of the forest.

3

Circa 1768

The years passed quickly and Calum, reaching the age of 17, grew to be a strong handsome young man and was a source of pride to his parents. Now that he was old enough to understand, they told him of the circumstances surrounding his birth and, upon hearing that they had taken him as their son, Calum gently pulled John and Jean into his broad arms and, hugging them both, quietly told them that he had always considered them to be his parents and what they both meant to him. He began working alongside John and absorbed everything that he was taught.

He was such a wonderful apprentice that John felt his son, who was now approaching 18 years of age, was going to be a better silversmith than he ever was. Word soon spread throughout the districts of his artistry and original designs, so much so that the business was finding difficulty keeping up with requests for their jewellery from the local gentry, thus giving the family a very comfortable income.

Calum began to set his mind on very intricate and delicate work, but always careful not to waste any of the precious metals and stones which were left in his charge. Over the months, one thought kept pressing through his mind, he pictured creating a piece so unique and original that, over the years, it would have a true meaning, but for the present, that meaning escaped him.

One evening, thinking along those lines, he recalled a day in the forest, when he was walking with his father and saw the most beautifully coloured butterfly sitting on a flower with wings outspread, as though it was willing the world to look upon his grandeur. This was to become Calum's obsession, to capture the beauty and serenity of that butterfly and mould it into his finest creation, knowing that it would surpass all the others that he had ever designed.

The following day he began the profile. Then, over the coming weeks, all his spare time was taken up concentrating on the precise interlacing on the inside of the profile with fine threads of precious metals, until all that was left to be done, was to insert the large piece of topaz in the centre of the jewel. Now that his task was ended, he gently picked up the brooch, as though it was a strand of fine gossamer, and held it in front of the glow emanating from one of the candles that lit up the room. Calum was taken aback by the richness of the colours, they seemed to mesmerize him, to the extent that he expected the butterfly to flutter its wings and soar off into the night. This was a moment that he would remember and cherish all the days of his life.

4

Murdoch Campbell with his wife, Catherine, and young daughter, Megan, along with his two young sons, had to flee from Inverness to escape the bloodbath that came after the defeat of the Jacobite rebellion. The Highlands were in complete turmoil and disarray. Not content with the victory over the rebels, the Duke of Cumberland, known throughout the country as the "butcher," oversaw the destruction of the Highland clans. He ordered Captain Henry St. Clair to take 50 dragoons and visit all the crofts and cottages nearest the battleground to search out the rebels with no mercy shown. All types of heinous crimes were committed in the name of the King, as they vented their hatred on innocent men, women and even children. This was a form of genocide and the beginnings of the Highland clearances.

The rain was torrential that morning, as the family were about to depart from the home where Megan had grown up. Her young heart was breaking as she looked on, watching her mother wring her hands in despair, while her tears, mixed with the rain, streamed down her face watching her husband load their meagre belongings onto a small horse-drawn cart. They were leaving behind the small holding that had been in their family for years. Murdoch felt angry and knew the hatred he felt inside for the English armies, would never leave him, but he also knew that the safety of his wife and children mattered most.

5

They set out for Edinburgh. This journey would take them almost a week to reach their destination and, being of modest means, they found it very difficult to find a suitable home compared to what they had left behind. However, they were fortunate to eventually find suitable accommodation in the poorer outskirts of the City. Murdoch found work as a labouring farmhand for a local farmer and, although he was only earning a pittance of a wage, it helped keep the wolf from the door.

Once a week, Megan and her mother would travel into the City to replenish some supplies and groceries. On one of these visits, they happened to stop outside the small silversmith shop to admire the fine trinkets in the window. The following month would be Megan's 18th birthday and, as was the custom in those times, it was seen to be a very special day in a girl's life and she was usually given a small gift from her parents. Because of the family's plight of not having much money, this was of grave concern for her parents, as they didn't want her to feel the hurt of disappointment.

When Megan and her mother entered the small shop, they were warmly greeted by Calum, who seemed transfixed from the moment he set eyes on Megan. She was petite and had a statuesque figure and her demeanour added so much to the elegance of her youthful beauty. The auburn ringlets of her hair framed her face, causing her dark hazel eyes to complement her dazzling smile. It was little wonder that, since her family had come to this part of the City, most of the young men who saw her were vying for her attention and, hopefully, her favours.

Realising that he was staring, Calum cleared his throat, trying to regain his composure, "Good morning ladies, may I be of assistance?" Megan appeared to blush, as she stepped demurely behind her mother and began browsing around the shelves, looking at all the fine pieces of jewellery on display. As there were other people milling around inspecting the fine pieces, her mother spoke quietly, appearing to be somewhat embarrassed, having to explain her financial situation. This had to be done before asking Calum if there was anything that he could show her which would accommodate her meagre budget, since this was to be a gift for her daughter, whose 18th birthday was on the Friday of the following month.

While Calum and Mrs. Campbell were discussing the costs of certain items, Megan was discreetly observing the young jeweller. What a handsome young fellow, so polite and soft spoken, not like her rough and ready sibling brothers, whom she usually had to watch over to keep them out of trouble. "Yes, I like this young man," she thought to herself.

After a short while, Calum found a delicate necklace with a pearl droplet hanging from a silver chain, which was more expensive than what was within Mrs. Campbell's price range, but he pretended it was just a simple piece.   As the gift was wrapped and they were about to leave the shop, Calum knew within his heart that he just had to meet this girl again, but how? Then it came to him, "May I have your address for my receipt ledger please?" On being given this information, he now knew where Megan lived, but there was still the problem of finding a way to see her.

6

Calum, meanwhile, had put it out of his mind until early the following month, as he made his usual journey to the shop, he heard someone call out his name. It was young Rab, the cobbler's son. "You'll be goin' tae the Ceilidh on Friday night, ah suppose? It's bein' held in old MacPherson's barn, so maist o' the lads an' lassie's will be there." Calum was about to say he would think about it, but then the answer to his problem, of meeting Megan, unfolded - he could make up some sort of excuse to see her and ask her to go to the Ceilidh with him. He then remembered her mother telling him that it was her daughter's birthday on Friday, so now his plan was formulated.

Later that evening, after closing the shop, he made his way to Megan's home, but upon arriving at the door, he had second thoughts, was this the proper thing to do, what if she said no, how foolish would that make him feel? He was about to turn around and walk away, when the door opened and there was Megan's mother standing with a broom in her hand, for a moment Calum imagined that he was about to be attacked by the broom, but her mother had come out to clear the snow from the door. "Oh" she exclaimed, "You're the young man from the jewellery shop, is there something wrong?" "No, Mistress MacGregor," he nervously blurted out. "I just wanted to give your daughter a small gift for her birthday and also to be so bold as to ask if you would be so kind and consent to letting me take her to the Ceilidh on Friday night." She smiled and said "Come on in laddie an' ye can ask her yersel'. You're all she's spoken about since we left your shop."

Then, before lifting the remaining dinner dishes and going into the small kitchen, she called out "Megan there's someone here to see you." When Megan came into the room and saw him standing there, her astonishment soon gave way to a delighted smile, as she asked "What are you doing here?" Calum reached into his pocket and brought out a small box. "This is a small birthday gift for you and I should be happy to see it worn by the beautiful girl that I pray shall accompany me to the Ceilidh come Friday night." Megan gasped in surprise, before saying "Thank you, that is ever so sweet of you," and her look of appreciation made Calum's heart jump. Upon opening the box, she found the most charming silver bracelet, studded with small glittering stones of many different colours. She was so taken by the surprise, she was lost for words, then, as she removed bracelet from the box and placed it on her wrist, she became so excited, she left Calum standing in the room, as she hurried to show the gift to her Mother and to also ask if she could go to the Ceilidh.

Her Mother was overjoyed by seeing how happy and excited Megan was and she knew in her heart it would be right for her to have some happiness in her young life, after the traumas of the past year. She also thought of how her daughter never complained about her many chores, or the time that she had to spend watching over and caring for her two younger brothers, so, without a moment's hesitation, she gave her permission. Coming back into the room, Megan couldn't hide how thrilled she was by the two wonderful surprises that she had received and, as she walked Calum to the door, she stopped in the small hallway to say, "Thank you for that precious gift, I'll always treasure it."

The days weren't passing fast enough for Calum, all he could think about was seeing Megan and, somehow, he felt that, since the moment he first met her, his life had taken on a new meaning. Was it fate that guided them to his shop... if so, it couldn't have been planned more perfectly, they both had discovered an instant attraction to each other and, now that he had the chance to be with her once more, life was just beginning.

7

On Friday night, Calum arrived to escort Megan, only to find the door opened by her father. Like most fathers throughout the ages, he wanted to inspect the man who was about to take his daughter to the Ceilidh. Upon being invited into the house, Calum followed Megan's father into the small kitchen to begin answering all the usual questions about where he lived, what he did for a living and so on. His answers seemed to meet with her father's approval, although he was told, in no uncertain terms, to have Megan back home before 10 p.m.

The sound of laughter and music filled the cold night air but, just as they approached the barn, Calum could feel her grasp his arm tightly, as though she was in need of his reassurance, he also noticed the uncertainty in her eyes from the noise emanating from the shouting and the skirling bagpipes and fiddle music that filled the cold night air, "Are ye' alright Megan, are ye cauld?" "No," she replied, "it's just that this is the first Ceilidh I've ever been to and besides, I can't dance." "Dinna worry lass, your feet will be tired afore this night's over."

Calum could see all the boys staring at his lovely young lady, the moment they walked through the door, and he knew it would only be a matter of time before they would be pushing and jostling each other to be the first to ask her for a dance, but, he was adamant he wouldn't let her leave his side. Their very first dance together was a slow strathspey and he was taken aback at how quickly she learned, he also noticed how nimble she was when they took part in a very fast eighth-some reel. His friend, young Rab, came over to ask if he could he have a dance with Megan and Calum relented, after all it was Rab who gave him the answer of how to meet Megan once more. As he looked on, watching Megan dance, he knew within his heart that he wanted to go through life with this beautiful girl. When the dance finished, Megan walked back to him. Calum could see the happiness she discovered by taking part in the reels and all the other dances "I'm so happy, I believe I could go on dancing forever," she said, looking into his eyes, and, as she took his hand entwining his fingers with hers, Calum responded, "If only we could, but I promised your Father I would have you back by ten, so we'll have to leave now."

Saying their goodnights to the others, they strolled home under a panorama of stars which shone through the thin veil of wintry clouds, allowing the translucence of the moonlight to cause the falling snow particles to glitter, as they fell to the ground, giving the appearance of a diamond studded carpet. This did not escape the young couple, as they both seemed to feel this night was made for them. However, they never really noticed the beauty of the enchantment, as they only had eyes and thoughts for each other. Arriving at Megan's door, Calum knew that he must see her again, so here was his chance to find out. "Megan, I have tae go and deliver a piece of jewellery tae a lady in the village of Roslin on Sunday and I was hoping that you could find the time tae come along?" "I'd be

14

most happy to and I don't think my Faither would object," she smiled, overjoyed to be with him again. "That's grand. I'll call for you at 1 o'clock and, Megan; I do look forward to seeing you again." In saying that, he placed his hand under her chin and raised her lips and kissed her ever so gently.

On Saturday, the hours seemed to drag by, as he couldn't contain his longing to see her again; he found it quite strange that he had never known such feelings of happiness, or anticipation, as he had now. Setting out on Sunday morning at 11 o'clock, in the small pony and trap that he had hired for the journey, he arrived at Megan's home. As she came out of the house to meet him, at first glance he was astounded by her loveliness. She wore a red plaid dress bordered by a lace neckerchief, showing off the necklace that her parents had purchased for her birthday. He also noticed that she was wearing the bracelet given to her by him. As he took her hand to help her into the seat of the carriage, he whispered into her ear "You look sublime." "Thank you kind Sir, this is another first for me, I've never been driven anywhere before." "Megan, I pray that you shall always permit me to be the one to show you all things that are new to you." After saying that, Calum felt he had overstepped the mark and felt like biting his tongue off. "I might just hold you to that," she coyly replied, smiling as she looked down at her feet so that he wouldn't see her blushing.

Upon their arrival at the village of Roslin, Calum delivered the package, before driving to a small Inn on the outskirts of the village.

This was where he was going to treat Megan to lunch. When he took her hand to help her out of the carriage, he felt her squeeze his hand, as she murmured, "You never fail to surprise me. Again, this is all new to me, another first. I've never been taken to dinner before." "This is another part of my birthday gift to you, and it's a small price to pay to have you here beside me." He smiled as he interlocked her fingers with his, holding her hand across the table.

After a lovely warm meal, they walked down to the North Esk River, which runs just below the village. There they strolled, hand in hand, along the footpath until they came within sight of the Roslin Chapel. As they stood admiring the old Chapel, Calum was about to say it was time for them to leave but, as he was about to speak, he was once more struck by her beauty. It was at this moment, he knew he wanted to make her his wife.

When they arrived home, he walked her to the door and, taking her hands in his, he looked into her eyes, and confessed "Megan, I've only known you for a few short weeks, but I can't get you out of my mind. This may sound strange, but I love you and want to marry you." Upon hearing this, she was lost for words, as her head was in a whirl. "I'm sorry Megan if I sounded blunt, but I had tae let you know how I feel. Please forgive me if I have caused ye' any embarrassment." She stood silent for a few moments before regaining her composure to answer his request "Oh yes, Calum, yes, I'll gladly be your bride." The words weren't out of her mouth before she found herself locked in his arms and being kissed passionately. This was another first for her and one that she would come to relish. Their first concern was how Megan's parents would react upon being told that she wanted to wed Calum. Their worries were unfounded as her Mother and Father were overjoyed upon hearing that she was marrying a young man of Calum's stature.

When old John heard the news of his son's impending marriage, he did a small jig of delight before shaking Calum warmly by the hand. "A'm happy for ye' son, thon wee lassie's getting a guid man an' ye both hae mah blessins."

The next day, unbeknownst to Calum, John set about the task of making a pair of gold wedding rings for the young couple, as this would be part of his wedding gift to them. Weddings were always seen as important rituals, so new clothes for the bride and groom had to be made, or purchased, as wedding attire for both the bride and groom was an integral part of the festivities. Marriages were about the exchange of property between both families, many weddings highlighted overt displays of wealth, thus making the bride's dress an easy way to underscore one's riches.

A show of extravagance was the furthest thing on Calum and Megan's minds, as their only concern was to have a simple wedding, which would appear to not be too extravagant. The ceremony was set for the first Sunday of the following month, giving both their families a few weeks to organize the event and, upon hearing the good news of the wedding, all their friends and neighbours couldn't wait to wish them long life and happiness in their marriage.

8

Before they knew it, the big day was upon them. No one expected the Church to be full, but as Megan walked down the aisle on her Father's arm to stand beside Calum, the Church was overflowing by friends and local customers, who had, at one time or another purchased their fine jewellery from the shop and they now came to offer their best wishes.

Megan was a vision of loveliness as she stood waiting to take her marriage vows. Her dress was white, which portrayed joy, not purity, that being represented by the blue band at the hem of her dress. One of the customs was that under her veil, which hid her from the spirits until safely in her husband's care, she wore a small wreath of wild forest flowers on her head. Another old custom was that, upon leaving her parent's house to make her way to the Church, the bride-to-be would have to step over piles of broken crockery because, on the eve of her wedding, friends and family would gather any old pieces of dishes or glass and place them outside the bride's door for good luck.

Before leaving the house to meet his bride, Calum's father asked him to sit for a moment and, as he sat facing his father, old John handed him the keys of the house saying, "This is my special gift tae you and

Megan, and I wish you all the happiness that this hoose gave me an' yer mither, ah know she would go alang wi' that." Although Calum was overwhelmed and taken aback at this generous offer, he at once refused. "I cannae accept that faither," Calum replied, "I'm sure Megan and I wouldn't mind stayin' under your roof until we get a wee place o' our own, that would be fine, but we wouldn't want to disrupt you, at this stage of your life, and besides that, where would you live?" John put his hand on Calum's shoulder "Hear me oot son, this hoose is too big for me noo, it's better suited fer a young family, an' anyways, ah need some time tae ma'sel so ah'll be goin' doon tae mah wee cottage at the coast tae stay, as ah' could dae wi' a wee break." Calum knew his Father would never take no for an answer and he really meant it, as he said "I'll never be able tae thank ye' enough faither, even if it took a lifetime." "Dinna fash yourself laddie, watchin' you grow up tae the man ye've become, was all the thanks yer mither an' I needed."

9

After the wedding vows were exchanged, the bride and groom sealed the marriage by drinking some wine from a small Quaich, which was commonly known as the loving cup and, when that was over, the ceremony was finalised.

On leaving the Church, the wedding procession was led by a fiddler and, when reaching Calum's father's house, Megan danced the wreath dance, which was often called "Dancing the bridal crown," with the wreath symbolizing her maidenhood. Married women danced around her, until the circle was broken by their fatigue, or intruding groomsmen, who then stole the wreath. Guests would try to take home a part of the broken wreath, which meant they would be married within a year. Another old wedding custom was for the best man to steal the bride, leaving the husband to find her. Usually these events could turn bawdy, which was part of the wedding ritual, but was all done in good humour.

As most of the guests dispersed back to their homes, the task was now up to Calum to find his bride. Little did the others know that one of the groomsmen had told him where the best man was hiding Megan. So, Calum made it appear that he was not sure where she was, he wasted some time looking here and there for her and, upon rescuing his new bride, the celebrations began anew with some of Calum's friends encircling Megan and dancing a reel with her in the centre. It was soon time for the newlyweds to leave. They tried to steal away unnoticed and as fast as possible, only to be spotted, with their departure being followed by a few bawdy innuendoes from the younger men who had stayed behind.

To Calum it seemed an eternity before they got to the front door of their new home and, upon entering, they were surprised to find a peat fire burning in the hearth and a few candles burning on the shelf above the fireplace, causing a warm glow throughout the room. Walking into the bedroom, they saw that the wedding bed had been turned down and a "warming pan" placed under the covers to preheat the sheets. Calum realised that some of their friends had prepared it especially for them. They stood in silence for a few moments, nervous and unsure of themselves in this situation He, because what he knew about love-making, he had gleaned from friends of what was expected of him on this special night; and, she was a bit fraught with anxiety, as she anticipated what was about to take place, but both their doubts vanished as Calum reached out and pulled her to him saying, "I love you Megan Campbell, an' ah want you to have this as a token of my love and I pray that, if we have a son, this shall be your wedding gift to him to pledge his love to his new bride." As he pinned the Topaz Butterfly on Megan's gown, his hand brushed against her breast, sending her senses reeling, she felt as though a fire was burning within her, this was all so new to her and she wanted more. With the next kiss, he pulled her tightly against his chest and, at that moment, she knew that she was prepared to surrender herself completely to his innermost desires. She broke away from him and, smiling shyly, asked if she could be excused for a few minutes to change her garments. He nodded and, when she went into the small ante-room, he strode over to the bed, removed his shirt, kilt and boots then he lay across the bed.

He heard Megan returning to the room, whereupon he immediately sat up on the bed. He watched as she stood perfectly still, undoing the ribbons that were fastened at her throat, allowing her gown to fall to the floor to reveal her slender, beautifully sculpted body. She felt slightly uneasy, as Calum rose from the bed, but her fear was quickly dispelled when he framed her beautiful face between his hands and, looking deeply into her soulful green eyes, he moved closer, before nudging his nose with hers, then he nipped at her lower lip before sliding his tongue deep into her eager mouth, igniting a fire within her. Every nerve in her body seemed to come alive and, as shivers of these unknown feelings tickled the surface of her skin, she rewarded him by moaning with pleasure. Her breathing became rapid and heavy and her moans were now barely audible. Her lips, which Calum had been savouring earlier, were now being devoured by him. Her small mouth was soft and warm and tasted sweet from the wine, which they both had previously sipped from the silver loving cup, sealing their marriage vows. He then slid his tongue along her lower lip and licked it lightly and, as he did so, she met his tongue with her own, opening her mouth slightly to let his tongue penetrate her pink hot mouth deeper, letting their tongues meet and flick against each other in a delicate dance. As they explored each other's oral cavities, he felt her put her arms around his waist, moaning softly before placing her hand on the back of his neck to cover his face with kisses. Pulling her body closer, he slid his hand up her rib cage and cupped her breast in his hand, flicking his thumb over the tip of her nipple, until it was hard enough to draw into his mouth, where he began to tease it with his tongue. Responding to the feathery touch of his tongue on her sensitive bud, Megan felt a warmth building up between her legs and. with each suck on her breast, increased her need. She heard herself gasp, as she felt his fingers move up her inner thigh, to caress her in such an enticing, seductive way, before nudging her legs apart, then placing his body down on hers. She couldn't find the words, but her body was screaming out for what she wanted. As he slowly joined his body to hers, uniting them as one, she could feel his hardness, causing her to pull Calum more deeply into her. He then began thrusting more ferociously, but stopped when he heard Megan cry out, as he tore through her maidenhead. The sharp pain suddenly eased and Megan began stroking his face, before asking "Why have ye' stopped?" "Ah didn't mean tae hurt ye, Megan, I heard ye cry out." "It was nothing dearest, now I'm a complete woman, your woman," and, in saying that, she enfolded him in her arms and wrapped her legs around his waist.

The next time she cried out was when he gripped her by the hips and plunged deep inside her, calling out her name, as he seemed to spasm and shudder. Megan felt the glow of pleasure and satisfaction as he emptied himself within her. She then lay ensconced in his arms, with her head resting upon his chest, sated and overcome in such a way that she never could possibly have imagined, and savoured the contentment that she felt in his arms, by the gentle stroking of his hand on her skin. When he began to move away, it seemed that he was taking a part of her with him. She closed her eyes, until he returned with a damp cloth and washed her body with such tender and passionate strokes. When it came time for him to come back to bed, she was now eager and willing to surrender to his every wish.

As the days passed, their love knew no bounds and they both had a holiday in their hearts when they were together. Life was sweet, filled with happiness and good fortune. Calum's prowess as a fashion jeweller became known throughout the city, and his business was growing busier by the day. However, with his Father no longer being there to assist in the running of the shop, it was becoming difficult to keep up with demands.   On the way home that evening, Calum's thoughts kept returning to the dilemma that was caused by being successful in business.

After supper that evening, he shared his concern with Megan, seeking her advice on how he could overcome this problem, which had been building up over the last few months. It had become apparent, with his father no longer being there to assist in the running of the shop; it was difficult to keep up with demands. After mulling this predicament over with Megan, trying to find a solution, they found the perfect answer. Why not approach her father and ask if he would consider the position of the daily running of the shop, then Calum could also employ her young brother to serve his apprenticeship as a silversmith and, whenever the need arose, make any deliveries to the customers.

Leaving the Church after the Sunday church service, they paid their usual visit to Megan's parents, only this time it was more than a social visit. Calum was prepared to make a monetary offer, which would prove beneficial to all of them. When Calum outlined his plan, her father didn't hesitate to accept what he found was a most generous and suitable opportunity for both him and his son, saying that he would start working at a moment's notice.   Now he could do a decent day's work, instead of the menial tasks he was doing as a farmhand.

10

With the new workers in place and doing what was required, Calum made the effort to spend more time with his beloved Megan, as it was always in the back of his mind that he was, in some ways, neglecting her by the number of hours he worked in the shop. Having the extra help now, he would make up for what they had been missing; most of all, Calum felt guilty by not keeping in touch with his father, especially when he would recall the fun-filled days of his youth and the wonderful loving upbringing both his parents shared with him. He knew that his father, being such an independent man, would never admit how lonely he must be feeling by staying all alone at his house on the coast. There was also the fact that he was now in his 80s and he was finding it more difficult to cope.

Calum took it upon himself to show his appreciation for the carefree life that his Father had given him as a boy, and how much Megan held his father in the highest esteem, so his first thought was to surprise her by posing his request to take his father under their roof. This would be an act of kindness, which, in a way, would also help thank him for all that he had done for them in the past. He also knew that Megan would warm to his idea of letting his father reside with them, as she liked nothing better than to listen to his stories, regaling her with his fond memories of the times spent with his young son.

Calum may have thought his suggestion would be a pleasant surprise to Megan. However, she turned the tables on him, with her very own surprise, the moment she smiled and replied, "That's wonderful dear, which means he'll be here for the bairn's arrival." Calum's eyes widened and his jaw dropped as he uttered "Ye' mean, Ye' mean..." "Aye! Ye're goin' tae be a Father." He rushed to Megan and swept her up into his arms and, as her feet left the floor, he twirled her in circles, before suddenly stopping and sitting her down on a chair exclaiming, "Whit ah'm a thinking of lass, in your condition ye shouldna' be getting excited like this." "Dinna be daft love, ah'm no made o' glass, ah'll no break." Like all new and expecting Fathers, Calum was full of questions, "When is the baby due? Would you like a boy or a girl?

Later that night, they called into Megan's parents' home to break the wonderful news and, upon hearing of the young couples' good fortune; her parents were overjoyed as they looked forward to the birth of their first grandchild. Megan's mother asked all the exact same questions that Calum had, as her father poured a dram and raised a glass to toast the expectant parents. Calum couldn't wait to break the news to his father. So, the next morning, he left the workshop in the capable hands of his father-in-law and set out early to make the journey to the cottage, with the intention of bringing his father back home.

When he arrived at the cottage, Calum stood at the picket fence and admired the well-maintained garden and lawn, remembering how, as a young boy, his father would give him seeds to plant, or let him water the flowers, then they would walk the short distance to the beach, where he would play on the sand, or splash his feet against the oncoming waves. Now, all that was left were those memories of his fun-filled days. When old John opened the cottage door to find Calum standing there, he pulled him into his arms saying "Oh my boy! It is wonderful tae see ye, but where's Megan?" When he was told the reason she was at home, and that he was going to be a grandfather, his eyes filled with tears. "This is the moment that I've looked forward tae and now I can die a happy man. Now tell me Son, when will the babby be born?" On being told of when the baby was expected, Calum then asked John if he would he consider returning home to stay and settle in with himself and Megan. At first, John was a bit reluctant, as he thought there may be a chance he would become a hindrance, but after some gentle persuasion from Calum, he relented and accepted the kind offer. This was only on the condition that he could assist with any chores that would help Megan. "That's whit ah want tae hear faither, now gather yer things taegither an' we'll be on oor way."

When Old John arrived home with Calum, he felt as though he had never left, especially by the welcome that met him, as he stepped through the door. Megan hugged him lovingly, before leading him by the hand to the large sitting room, where her parents were also there on hand to greet him. Sitting down to a wonderful meal, the night was then spent in jovial conversation. Nights like these helped keep both families in constant touch, and Megan's mother promised to stay in close contact with her daughter during her confinement. This was much appreciated by Calum, when she assured him she would arrive daily and stay, giving Megan as much support and assistance, as she was needed nearer the time for the birth of her first grandchild.

As the months rolled by, John noticed a change in Calum, he sensed a mood of anxiety had taken over from the promising outlook of becoming a father, only to be replaced by the gradual worrying thoughts of all things that could go wrong, when Megan was about to give birth. Megan's pregnancy was almost full-term and Calum was beginning to fear for her health. She was just a slip of a girl and her body was heavily swollen with child. He knew the risks of childbirth and what could happen at the critical stages of a child being brought into the world. The chances of women not living through childbirth were between 1 and 2 percent.

11

Scotland was becoming more populated and crowded in the 17th and 18th Centuries and there were communicable diseases causing most deaths in childbirths than any other. Puerparal fever and squalid living conditions took their toll as the rise of physician-assisted births increased, so also did the death rate. This was a bacterial infection which became apparent within days of giving birth. The doctors were unaware of the germs and bacteria they were carrying on the instruments and unwashed hands. Women faced birth, not with joy, but with uncertainty and the fear of death. Hence the reason for Calum being so forlorn and, based upon these facts, he knew it was imperative to have Megan's mother present to be with her daughter when the time came.

Catherine was well-versed on what to do, as she had often been present at other births and gained experience by helping some of the other women in the village bring new life into the world. She had often assisted in the birthing of many a calf on her husband's small farm, so her expertise, though limited, would suffice in helping Megan go through this unknown in her life as smoothly and painlessly as best she could. Each night, when he returned home from the shop, Calum would sit by Megan's bedside telling her all the latest news that he had heard on what was taking place daily and how friends and neighbours were sending their best wishes. As he sat holding her hand, he felt helpless, as he knew that very soon she would be having excruciating pain throughout her traumatic ordeal and he began feeling distraught when he realized this was her unfair reward for loving him.

Suddenly, her breathing became shallow and Calum felt her fingers grasp his hand in a vice-like grip, as she told him to call for her mother. The moment Catherine entered the room and caught sight of how pale and wan Megan's skin was, and her eyelids, when closed, appeared translucent. She knew the baby was due any moment now, so she quickly filled the large cast iron pot and attached it to the metal hook above the open fire. She then set about gathering an armful of towels, which were prepared previously, and she set them on the bottom of the bed.

She helped Megan sit up and placed her legs over the edge of the bed, thus making it easier for Megan to stand, alleviating her labour pains, which were crushing her swollen belly every few minutes. Catherine then went outside and told Calum to quickly summon one of the women from the village to come and assist her, as she feared this was going to be a very long and sleepless night for all of them. While waiting for some outside help, Catherine applied cold wet towels to her daughter's forehead, which seemed to help bring down the fever that was permeating Megan's slight frame. Catherine instructed Megan to begin counting from one to whatever number she reached, when a labour pain attacked. Megan would reach twenty-eight, at which time the pain appeared to subside. She continued counting as her mother held her hand throughout the crucial seemingly unending hours. Megan's mind was in turmoil, she was afraid at the thought of what if something dreadful happened to her, or the baby, how would Calum cope? Suddenly, she felt such a ferocious pain, it seemed to tear her body apart, she had never experienced such agony and now, when the pain wracked her tortured frame, she prayed for this torment to end. Calum was becoming more worried and anxious as he stood waiting outside the bedroom door. "Whit's happening in there faither?" "Ah cannae say son, ah only know she's in good hands an' all we can do is wait an' let nature tak' its course."

The atmosphere in the bedroom was becoming tense, as Megan's mother monitored Megan's contractions and also the baby's position and location in the birth canal (most all babies' heads enter the pelvis facing to one side and then rotate to face downwards), although often a baby will be facing upwards, towards the mother's abdomen. Intense back pains can also incur with this position. The midwife may try to rotate the baby, or the baby may turn naturally, as nature had intended, now, as she was nearing the end of her first stage of labour, Megan's contractions became longer, stronger and closer together. Catherine urged her to try lying in different positions, as she began rubbing Megan's lower back in a bid to help ease the severe labour pains, then gave her sips of cold water, before placing cold compresses on her forehead. As the contractions progressed, Catherine could see her daughter was going into the second stage of delivery. This is when the contractions became very powerful, causing Megan to feel nauseous and began shivering uncontrollably. Catherine placed another blanket over her daughter, in a bid to keep her warm. This part of the birthing processes involves pushing and usually lasts between 20 minutes and 2 hours, then the delivery of the baby. Megan was urged periodically to push really hard, then rest between the contractions.

At this stage Catherine asked Calum to fetch Mrs. Tufts, a woman from the village, who had assisted at many previous births, to help Megan become focused on the pushing and help her find the most comfortable position in which to deliver her baby. As the night wore on, the pain overtook Megan, leaving her physically exhausted, but

Catherine and Mrs Tufts could see that the baby's head was crowning and urged Megan to exert one last mighty push, then, summoning up all her strength, she obeyed her mother and, all at once, there was a loud wail as Calum and Megan's son entered the world. Scooping the baby up, Catherine wrapped him in a large towel and handed him to Mrs. Tufts to clean him off, as she cut the umbilical cord. Megan's contractions continued for an additional 30 minutes after the baby was born, but gladly the labour pains subsided and were gone.

Catherine bustled about and asked Megan that, once she was properly cleaned, to sit in the large chair, whilst she changed the bed linen. She also assured Megan that her son was a perfectly healthy baby and how the rest of the family will be so happy for her and Calum. In the meantime, Calum and his father were pacing about outside in the cold night air, anxious to hear how things were coming along, but there wasn't a sound to be heard. Calum, as big and strong as he was, found himself quaking inside, as he hoped and prayed that all was going well. Suddenly, the front door opened and there stood Megan's mother, with a beaming smile "Come inside laddie and meet your bonnie son." Calum could feel his heart beating as though ready to explode, as he rushed into the bedroom and, the moment he caught sight of the little baby lying cradled in the crook of Megan's arm, his eyes welled up with tears of joy and relief, knowing that his wife and child were both fine. Calum sat on the side of the bed and softly stroked Megan's face as he looked into her tired eyes, "We have a beautiful son and I have surely been doubly blessed, thank you my love," he whispered, as he kissed her smiling lips. Catherine lifted the baby and brought him to Calum "Hold your son, father, and then we'll let his mother have a much, deserved rest." The baby looked so small and fragile, thought Calum, as he cradled him in his strong arms, although somehow in that instance of seeing the child look so weak and helpless, something inside told him that this tiny boy would become a man of stature. Over the weeks that were leading Megan back to full health, they decided on naming their son Charles, after the "Young Pretender" and he was christened in the old Kirk where they had wed.

12

Circa 1770

When Charles was 5 years of age, Calum could afford to have the boy tutored at home.   Charles soon became adept at both Greek and Latin languages and, upon reaching the age of 8, he was reading the Classics. It wasn't all work and no play, as every weekend he and his grandfather would make the short journey to the cottage on the coast. There, he would while away the hours at the Leith dockside, doing what he loved best, watching the tall ships being replenished with food for the crew and all types of cargo being loaded on board. He found an unusual air of excitement listening to sailors from different parts of the world talking in their native language, or he would stand for hours looking on at a ship becoming a faint dot, as it faded over the horizon and imagining how it must feel to be part of that crew sailing off to strange lands.

The older Charles became, the more his attraction to the sea took hold, until he knew he must surrender to his obsession to sail before the mast.

One weekend, after returning home from the cottage, Charles struggled with his dilemma and felt a pang of guilt as he thought of the sadness and heartache that he may be causing his parents if he left, after the wonderful education and home life that they had given him. Now, here he was on the verge of asking their permission to leave the house that held so many happy memories for the family. After much soul searching, he decided that the best way to broach the subject was to wait until after the evening meal when his parents would be together, and that would be the opportune time to declare his intentions of enlisting in the navy.

As they all sat in the glow of the open fire, Calum smiled as he turned to Charles saying "Ah have a wee surprise for ye' son, noo that you're nearly 15, ah think it's aboot time ye should be learnin' the first steps o' the silversmith trade." At hearing those words, Charles felt as if he had been stabbed through the heart, then what followed was a numbness, which ran through his entire body, but he knew that he must declare his dream before his father made any more plans for his future. "Father, you must forgive me for not telling you sooner, but I have a strong desire to join the Navy, hopefully, as a Midshipman as a junior officer then, with God's grace progress to a higher rank." As he listened to his son, Calum's mind was in turmoil and, as he turned to Megan, he could see her eyes well up, before she averted his gaze. This was so unexpected, what should he say or do for that matter? After the shock had worn off, he could see the disappointment in his son's eyes that he might not get his father's permission, or blessing, to follow his dream. "Ah'll have tae think aboot it, but ye'll have tae bide by mah decision."

Over the next few days, Calum pondered over this dilemma and even confided in his own father, John, who advised him not to stand in the boy's way, as you can't force him into something that he doesn't care for.   He even told Calum he could see the happiness that Charles found, whenever they were on the shore, watching the ships as they were outward bound. After listening to old John, Calum realised it would be fruitless to refuse his son his wish, as the last thing he wanted was to dampen the boy's spirit. The next day, he told Megan the reason for his decision and, even though she put on a brave face, he could see the sadness in her eyes. "Ah'll sorely miss him, Calum, especially him being so young, he's still a child and the hoose will seem empty withoot him." "That may be, dear, but it would be foolish tae refuse him, as we'd be taking away his dream, as his heart is set on a naval career and ah have no doubts, he'll do us proud."

Upon hearing their decision, old John didn't waste any time on contacting an old friend, whom he had known for many years and who happened to be a retired sea captain.   Upon being told of the situation, he assured John he would do his utmost to help his grandson and, true to his word, within days, he visited John with what was known as a letter from the Crown. These were instructions for whatever ship's Captain accepted Charles as a midshipman, to show kindness as they saw fit for a gentleman; to further his knowledge by assisting his learning in navigational mathematics - although this task was usually given to a senior master's mate. Along with the letter, John's friend also provided the name of an Inn, situated close to the dockside, and was known as the "Anchor Tavern." This was the haunt of sailors who were often prepared to spend whatever money they had left, drinking and carousing with the local prostitutes until they could find work on whatever ship that was sea bound, to earn some money before returning home to continue with the only sort of dismal life that they had ever known.

13

Two weeks after his 15th birthday, it was a sad and tearful farewell for his parents and grandfather, as they watched young Charles board the Mail coach, which was bound for Glasgow, taking him on the first steps to achieve his aim of becoming a Naval Officer.   Little did he know that this was the last time he would see his grandfather again, as old John succumb to a fatal bout of pleurisy, only to pass away three weeks after the boy had left.

When, after a long and tedious journey, the coach reached its destination, the passengers disembarked at 'The Saracens' Head Inn" which is situated in the East End of Glasgow. The Inn was a very popular place among travellers to Glasgow and no journey was seen to be complete without a visit to the Inn. Many famous literati rested under its roof, notably Robert Burns, Sir Walter Scott and William Wordsworth. The Inn was originally opened to the public in 1755, boasting 36 rooms and a ballroom that could accommodate one hundred dancers; it also had stables for sixty horses. Over the years, the ballroom and the stables were both demolished, leaving the Inn, which is still there to the present day, and is now used solely as a public house.

After a good night's rest, followed by a hearty breakfast, Charles paid a few pence to have the chest, which held all his worldly belongings, loaded onto a small wagon that would take him down to the river Clyde. There, he would seek out the tavern and hopefully find a berth on a ship that would be sailing for Portsmouth. Reaching the dockside just before noon, he was taken aback by the amount of noise coming from the people who appeared to be one crowded throng. This was all so new to him, considering the quiet lifestyle he had been accustomed to. There were street vendors crying out loudly to attract all and sundry, adding to the cacophony of the sounds that filled the air. There were also the beggars and street urchins being shouted at, to be chased away, as they jostled among the crowds, looking for some kind stranger to be charitable. Added to this, was the noise coming from the cartwheels as they rumbled noisily along the raised contours of the uneven cobblestones, as the carter skilfully manoeuvred the horses through the bustling throngs.

After wandering for what seemed an eternity, he, at last, found the ale house where the ships sailors gathered. On entering, it was so dark, he had to half close his eyes to become accustomed to what was happening around him and was surprised to find there were also women sauntering around, approaching anyone who appeared interested, or would buy them ale, by placing their arms around their necks, or by sitting on their knee. This certainly was another world to the boy, as he found himself surrounded by all sorts of people, the likes of whom he had only read of, so different from the sailors that he watched at the docksides of Leith. These men were rag tags, callous, loudmouth oafs who cursed repeatedly and most of them carried scars on their unwashed faces, due to drunken brawls no doubt. "What have we here then?" Charles was startled by the heavy hand gripping him by his shoulder. "You're a brave young cock to be strolling around this den of thieves, what's your business here boy?" Charles stood transfixed and felt his mouth go dry, as he looked up and into the face of this giant of a man whose eyes were cold, hard and unyielding, with a deep scar on his cheek, which ran from the lobe of his right ear to the corner of his mouth, allowing his lip to twist upwards in a sardonic grin. He was accompanied by two red-coated soldiers, and his rugged bearing clearly outlined that he wasn't one of the poor unfortunate miscreants who frequented this establishment. He wore a long blue brass buttoned naval coat, black knee length breeches and white hose with brass buckled shoes. Even for one so young, Charles knew this denoted naval attire. Lowering his wizened eyes towards Charles, the colossus peered into the boy's upturned face, stating "I take it you can talk, young man?" This shook the boy to the core, but he responded with all the courage he could muster, and he felt his face flush, as he replied in a strong voice, "Yes, Sir. I can." "Well, speak up, boy and tell me your tale." "My name is Charles Sinclair, I am 15 years of age and hail from the city of Edinburgh and wish to enlist in the King's navy with the sole intention of becoming a Midshipman. I have on my person a letter of the Crown for any Captain that sees fit to complement me as a member of his naval officers." The large man looked down at the boy and breaking into a twisted grin said, "I like the cut of your jib young'un and, if you care to anchor here for a short while, you can accompany me and the new crew to meet Captain Longworth of his Majesty's good ship H.M.S. Olympia. My name is Silas Bragg and I am the master mate, who, at this moment in time, is recruiting the latest contingent of riff raff to crew the Olympia and we shall be sailing on the morning tide, come rain or shine."

With that, he left Charles standing at the doorway, while he and the two soldiers, who strode behind him, went about their task of finding enough bodies to crew the Olympia. Silas Bragg sought out those who appeared to be the worse for drink and when they were approached and offered the King's shilling, they were quite happy to accept, as it meant another chance to drink. Others, on refusing or unwilling to become crew members, were quickly persuaded quite violently, before being dragged along by the callous and heavy-handed soldiers. One young man pleaded not to be taken, stating he had a wife and young baby at home, but Silas replied that this was his penance for getting married and was told to fall in with the rest of the unfortunates. Charles couldn't believe his eyes at the type of men that formed before him, some were so drunk they could barely stand, while others still attempted to escape from the Inn, but were held back at gunpoint by the soldiers, before being forced to walk with the others down to the ship, which was going to be their home for who knows how long. Silas could see the look of disdain on the boy's face, at the treatment that was being meted out to these unfortunate souls. "Don't think about them, my young cove, look to yourself lad and, mark my words, you won't find favour with any of these rascals, for as of now and as young as you are, you have authority over these men and they shall resent you for having unquestioned power at your disposal and would slit your throat at the drop of a hat."

Charles walked with him alongside one of the armed militia at the head of the procession, while bringing up the rear of these forlorn mendicants, was the second soldier who would look out for anyone that attempted to take a chance at making a bid for freedom. As they approached the dockside, to take their places in the longboats that would ferry them to the ship through the swirling mist, Charles could see the spectral outline of the "Olympia" that was anchored a good distance from the shore. Charles felt a current of excitement and, as he waited for the rest of the group to be gathered together, he suddenly began to shiver, was it the thought of the uncertainty of what lay in store, or the cold wind assaulting his body, he pulled his coat collar up to his ears, trying to ward off the gale force wind that seemed to be growing stronger. At last, he stepped aboard the longboat that would take him away from his family. These were the very same thoughts that he had and that's the moment he felt the first signs of being homesick. Charles pulled his heavy collar up around his ears, as he attempted to ward off the gale force wind. Casting off, the four oarsmen of the longboat strained every muscle as they fought against the howling wind and the choppy sea. They steered through the high waves towards the side of the vessel to where the "Jacob's Ladder", which consisted of flexible ropes supporting horizontal wooden rungs, which would be lowered for the crew to climb aboard.

As they approached the ship, Silas gripped the bottom rung of the ladder, doing his utmost to hold it steady from the force of the wind, and pulled it towards him, as he tried to judge the churning swell from the waves that were causing the small craft to rise and fall. This was making it difficult for the oarsmen to get their craft close to the side of the ship. As the longboat thumped noisily against side of the ship, Silas waited for the precise moment for the waves to bring them closer to the ladder then, gripping Charles by the shoulder and roaring above the sound of the wind, told him to be prepared for the next chance he got to step onto on first rung of the ladder. "You'll be leading the way boy, but be careful with your footing, we don't have the time to be pulling you from the water." Charles clutched both sides of the ladder, as it swung perilously from side to side then swinging outward, before the wind caused it to thud against the side of the ship and, with every step he took, he felt his insides churning at the thought of falling back into the longboat, which was now bobbing up and down, as the waves relentlessly appeared to be getting stronger.

At last, his ordeal was over, when he felt a rough hand grasp his wrist pulling him through a deck opening. "Welcome aboard, I'm Second Officer Beaton, I'll be taking stock of this newest batch of unwilling volunteers. I take it by your outfit and age that your wish is to serve as a Midshipman. Well for now, you can get out of those wet clothes and I'll get one of the men to show you to your quarters and get your chest with your dry clothes to you, as soon as possible. Your bunk is below the gun deck and that's where you'll be berthing, in the company of the other two new students."

As the remaining remnants of the downcast crew struggled aboard, Charles looked on and felt sorry for these pitiful forlorn souls, as he watched them being herded together, like obstinate cattle, these men were remnants from a lifetime of abject poverty. Most had sunken lifeless eyes, devoid of hope, with thin skeletal frames that came from a lifetime of being undernourished. Charles suddenly realised how cold he was but, unlike the poor unfortunates, he had a warm berth to look forward to. Above the noise that was coming from some of the leading hands, one of the crew instructed Charles to follow him. Making his way down to where he would be berthed, he was astounded to find that there were women on board ship. These were the wives of the regular crew, who were allowed to stay with their men before being put ashore when the ship was ready to sail.

Charles was taken down towards the stern of the ship by a sailor who pointed to a small door, "Here is your berth, remember we sail on the first tide." Upon entering the small dark room, Charles could make out three other young men, who, like him, wanted to become midshipmen, sitting around what appeared to be a table, which had a few candles that barely lit the room. They all appeared to be in the same age bracket as Charles and, after introducing themselves to each other, they were informed that they would be summoned to the Captain's quarters in the morning, so they had better bed down for the night. It was difficult to sleep in such cramped conditions, but the other lads were told previously that this small gunroom was only temporary until they set sail, and the womenfolk were offloaded.

They were awakened from their sleep, early the next morning, by the cacophony of sound, as the ship was getting ready to weigh anchor. Orders were being given to get the women off the ship and other officers were shouting above the noise to get the men to climb the rigging and undo the sails. Below deck, other sailors were scurrying about getting supplies in some semblance of order, as others carried out different chores. Sitting huddled over the table, the boys were relieved to hear a voice thunder out "Belay there ye' scurvy vermin, officer coming through." The noise died down, as Lieutenant Foster approached their makeshift table, "Come with me gentlemen, time to meet your Captain."

As they followed behind, Charles couldn't help but notice the unfriendly, sneering looks in the eyes of the sailors. He got the impression that they hated the authority that these young men would eventually have over them, but they also knew that to refuse orders could mean being hung from a yardarm. As they entered the Captain's quarters, Charles was taken aback by the size of the cabin. It was much smaller than he had imagined it would be. It was rather sparse with a long table, where all sort of charts were laid out and a small bookshelf filled with sea manuals. There were also a few chairs and, hanging from the ceiling were some Tilly lamps. As Charles stood to attention with the others, Captain Sinclair Tremayne paced back and forth, before addressing the young recruits. "Gentlemen, your first duty it to serve King and Country, then you must attain the rank of Deck Officer with a confidence that can be trusted, and with an assurance to make this vessel the scourge of the seas. Your first chore shall begin tomorrow by taking turns on watch with the Officer that you shall be assigned to. Thereafter, you shall be taught to use a sextant and read charts and become proficient with a compass. My Officers shall keep a record of your progress and report directly to me on how you are advancing. I trust you realise how fortunate you are to have such an opportunity, so use your free time well by listening and learning from the Officers. You can now retire to your berths and prepare for tomorrow, as we sail at first tide."

14

Charles heeded the Captain's advice, by studying hard in his free time, and set about any given task with such a zealous manner that, within six years, he was promoted to Deck Officer. Another two years passed and, due to his seamanship and the way that he handled the crew, he was promoted to Second Lieutenant. Seven years passed after he had attained his officer status, and, having taken part in many bloody and successful battles, he was once more promoted to Post Captain and given command of his own ship, which happened to be a frigate. This was a ship of the line, allowing him to capture enemy ships and share the money, which they received from selling the cargo, with his crew. He patrolled off the French coast for two years and was successful in capturing a fair number of cargo laden merchant ships, amassing a fair amount of money in the process.

Unfortunately, during a battle with a French corvette off the coast of Spain, his knee was shattered by a musket ball and, though badly wounded, insisted on staying with his men until the battle was won, only then did he allow himself to be carried by his officers to the Surgeon's table. Even then, he ordered the surgeon to care for those of his men who were more wounded than himself. Upon being examined, he was given the bad news that he would have to return home, otherwise, there was a strong chance of his leg having to be amputated. This news knocked the wind out of Charles and, although badly wounded and delirious at times, he knew the gravity of his injury. This was a catastrophic change and he realised that this would mean the end of his naval career, but he was desperate to reach his beloved home in Scotland.

15

However, this journey would be waylaid somewhat, as he was transferred to an English hospital in Netley (near Southampton) which was one of five military general hospitals in the U.K.   While there, the surgeons did what they could for Charles, cleaning the wound of foreign objects and fragments from his knee, while holding the bones together as best they could. The pain was excruciating and the medication, such that it was, didn't seem to alleviate the intensity of it. Charles tolerated the administration of dressing changes and bathing as best he could, but the nurses seemed to be run off their feet taking care of the other wounded officers and sailors.

There was one young nurse, Charlotte, who caught his eye. But, being a relatively new nurse, there was a "no nonsense" attitude about her. She knew that the Matron was keeping a sharp eye over her charges and, woe-be-tide anyone who showed favouritism to a patient. It was during the stillness of the evening, just after midnight, while most of the patients had settled down for the night, Charles needed to use the lavatory. He was struggling to sit up, when a sharp stab of pain shot through his body, making him cry out. Charlotte, who was the nurse on duty, ran to his bedside to assist him. Putting her arm around his shoulders, she helped him lay back on the pillows, and quietly told him not to move, that she would bring something to his bed, in order that he could use the commode. Charles was mesmerized by her gentle touch, yet her arms had a strength which belied her small frame, and the feelings that surged through his body, as she held him against hers, made him forget how much pain he was in. His mind was in a fog, yet he knew that this young nurse meant something to him. He also knew that there was some sort of connection between the two of them.

Once he was settled down for the night, he found he couldn't sleep. Thoughts of Charlotte were churning in his brain; closing his eyes willing himself to sleep, but to no avail. Time passed very slowly, when suddenly he felt a tap on his shoulder, Charlotte whispered to him, "Captain Sinclair, I have brought you a brew of tea, it may help you to sleep." Charles thought he was dreaming, but clearly this was not an apparition, this was his nurse dispensing a kindness, not afforded the other patients. Surely, this was a sign of affection, he thought. Putting this whimsical thought out of his mind, he thanked her and drank the potion slowly as she held the container, then he drifted off to sleep. The days passed abominably slow, and, in a very discreet manner, Charlotte administered aid to Charles in a caring manner, escaping the eagle eye of the Matron.

Charles knew that he should be returning home to his native country, Scotland, very soon. The surgeons concurred that, if his leg was to be saved, he would be safer in the hands of one of the skilled surgeons in Scotland, who were well suited to operating on his type of wound. However, he could not travel alone. This was when Charlotte was approached by the medical team in the hospital, to see if she would be willing to accompany Charles back, on the long journey to his homeland.

16

Circa 1795

It was settled. They both would have to travel to Scotland in a carriage, especially equipped to handle a special bed for Charles. Charlotte would make sure he was made as comfortable as possible. This journey would take many days and they would have to stop at certain Inns along the way, in order that Charles could get the appropriate rest, which was necessary for the special care for his injured leg. Their expenses had to be kept meagre, as they knew that they were limited to the funds, which were made available to them by the Naval Authorities, so they decided to register at the Inns as husband and wife. This would mean there would be less explanation to be given to the Innkeeper. At the first stopover, they settled into their room quite nicely, but the atmosphere was tense and conversation was strained, to say the least. Charles, who already knew that he was besotted by this young desirable woman, was reluctant to make the first move. Charlotte excused herself by saying she was going to get something for their supper.

While she was gone, Charles tried to prepare himself for bed before she returned.   He hated the fact that he was dependent on her for almost everything. He carefully put his crutches at the side of the bed, sat down and, somehow, his good leg slipped away from him and he fell on the floor in a heap.   Unable to get up, he started crawling towards his crutches. It was, at that moment, Charlotte returned. Seeing Charles in this predicament, she immediately dropped her purchases on the bed and ran to his side. Gathering him into her arms, she chided him, "Charles, what were you thinking?" Her hand went immediately to her mouth; she had called him by his first name. He saw how flustered this had made her, and he started laughing. Charlotte became indignant, as she struggled to regain her composure. "How dare you laugh at me, Captain Sinclair!" At that, he put his hand out to her and pulled her to his chest. "Charlotte, please let us stop this charade. You must know I have feelings for you, and, if I may be so bold, you possibly may reciprocate those feelings for me." As she lay there on top of his chest, her heart pounding against his, she uttered, in a small voice, "My dear Charles, you know me better than I seem to know myself. Yes, my feelings for you run deep, but I felt that this could possibly be a crush, on my part." Now that this secret had been revealed, Charles lifted Charlotte's chin, by his index finger and softly placed his lips upon her hers. Charlotte felt as though the room was spinning, as she eagerly responded to his kiss, and this warmth enveloped her body.

As they regained their composure, Charles, once again, was lying on the bed, but, he did not let go of Charlotte's hand...he wanted to share, in depth, what she meant to him. As they lay together, his arms clasping her to his chest, he asked her if she trusted him. "Implicitly, Charles. My feelings for you run so deep, it is a mystery to me. I have never known such emotions before," she responded, as the tears softly coursed down her delicate face. Charles hugged her harder, and said, "Charlotte, it is my dearest wish to ask for your hand in marriage, however, I would like for us to make plans for our wedding to be held in my home town, with my parents witnessing this blessed event. What do you say, my love?" She looked lovingly at his scars and pretended not to notice them, just as any decent person would have, and, as she nodded in the affirmative, his mouth covered hers, leaving her breathless. As their lips parted, his stare settled on her, and it was then he knew he could not wait any longer. It was hard to see his expression in the deep shadows, but he froze, and then he let his hands fall to his side.

He sat up on the edge of the bed and started to take off his boot, as his other leg was set in some sort of cast to keep the knee and lower rigid from any movement. Charlotte, by this time, rose from the bed and knelt at his feet, feeling the worn carpet under her stockings. Before he could get up from the bed, she stood up as he made his way to her. Standing so close, she felt her legs brush against his knees. She could hear his breathing, a little faster than normal. Then Charles tilted his head back to regard her. A sliver of light, from the outside, worked its way through the drapes and Charlotte could see his eyes searching her face. Lifting a trembling hand, she brushed the hair from his forehead. At her touch, he sighed and relaxed his shoulders. Charlotte drew Charles to her, resting his face against the soft fabric of her gown. Her palms slid over his back, feeling the warmth of his skin through his shirt. He slowly sat down on the bed once more, as Charlotte knelt before him and caressed his face. He closed his eyes when she touched him, allowing her to gently trace some of his slightly raised scars on his leg with her fingertips. She then ran the pad of her thumb over his bottom lip, aching for him to kiss her. It was as if Charles sensed her need. Taking her into his arms, so that her face was level with him, he pressed his mouth to hers. It was a gentle, chaste kiss, the kind she was not familiar with, then she wrapped her arms around his neck and they fell back against the bed. The kiss deepened and, when he opened his mouth to hers, she dared to slide her tongue inside. Charles moaned and slipped his arms around her waist, pulling her tighter to him. She felt an unfamiliar warmth between her thighs, the longing to be touched there. Rocking his hips against hers, his hand reaching between them to rest on her thigh. Charlotte broke the kiss, breathing heavily, "We shouldn't, Charles." Her words were tender, but they felt like a rebuke, and he sat up quickly saying, "I'm sorry, I shouldn't have done that." Charlotte grabbed his wrist with a firmness that made him pause, as she said, "What? No, wait; I don't want you to stop." His face burned with shame, "I hope you don't think this is something that I make a habit of doing. It is because I love you so much Charlotte. She let him ease her back onto the bed, saying, "Will you…. just lie here with me for a little while?"

Stretching out on the bedspread, he drew her close to him once again. "Are you cold?" he whispered, and she felt his lips brush the top of her head. "No," she whispered back, closing her eyes. She rested her hand on his chest, playing with one of the buttons on his shirt. "How old are you, Charles?" "I just turned thirty-one." He grew quiet for a minute, and then asked, "Does that bother you?" "No, why should it?" "Well, to be honest with you, it bothers me a bit," he said, "I'm nine years older than you." She swallowed hard, "Is that why you don't want to....? She left the rest of the question unspoken. "That's part of the reason, the main problem is that you would think less of me, because we are not married yet." "Darling, ease your mind, soon we will be wed and tonight we will pretend that we are," she coyly responded. Charles reached for her hand, and their fingers intertwined. She could feel a pulse where their skin touched, not knowing if it was his or hers.   Charles eased her down onto the bed, his arms around her. Charlotte rested her head on his chest and listened to the thump of his heart. "You have absolutely nothing to be ashamed of, Charlotte, because we are betrothed to each other, as of now, and we will be married as soon as we arrive at my parents' home in Scotland," he whispered in her ear. Her body responded to Charles' words, as if they were strokes on her skin. Her nipples hardened, and she felt a surge of heat between her thighs. She gazed at his full lips, wanting to kiss them, then began leaning towards him, searching to kiss his mouth.   The lamp in the room was turned down low, with only a few candles lit, giving the room some illumination. They lay together in each other's arms, when Charles continued fondling Charlotte's left breast, and he lowered his head to her right, taking the nipple between his lips, grazing it with the tip of his tongue. Charlotte slid her palms over his back, across his ribs, feeling as much of him as she could. She didn't think she'd ever grow tired of tracing her fingertips across his flesh. Moving her hands to the buttons on his trousers, Charles took over the task of removing the rest of his clothes. Their eyes met, and she smiled shyly, hiding the excitement she could barely contain. She wanted to throw herself at him, cover his body with hers, but Charles had other plans.

Once more, Charles gently laid Charlotte's back against the bed, and with his hands and mouth, he began a slow exploration of her body, like her skin was a map he wanted to memorize. He lingered over her breasts, drawing lazy circles around her nipples with his tongue, until she began to whimper, and then he sucked one into his mouth. Her muscles felt like they were melting in a pool of warmth. She could feel his erection against her thigh, and she tried to reach between them to stroke his manhood, but he raised his head and whispered, "Not yet. I just want to focus on you." Charles' mouth moved lower, and when he dipped his tongue into her belly button, she giggled. "Ticklish?" he said, grinning up at her. "I'll have to remember that." His hands slid over her hips and then to her thighs. Parting them gently, he noticed the two-inch scar a couple of inches above her right knee. "What happened here?" "I fell against a wall when I was ten."   Charles kissed the scar, and Charlotte's breath hitched in her chest, as his lips travelled further up her thigh. Gazing down at him, she was aware of how wet she'd already become. He inhaled deeply and closed his eyes, and then he used his tongue to part her outer lips. She gasped, propping herself up on her elbows, taking in the sight of him lying between her thighs, his hands grasping her hips. "You taste amazing," he whispered, and those words made her womanhood ache with need. She tugged at her nipples, the sensitive peaks hard between her fingers, and her arousal grew even more fervent. Charles ran his tongue along either side of her thighs before edging his tongue against her swollen labia. She released a low moan, as their combined wall shadows, cast from the bedside candles, gyrated in larger than life animation as she relished the sensation of his hot, wet mouth on her. He slipped a finger inside that most private of parts, so gently, then he gave her clitoris one rapid flick of his tongue, just to tease. She cried out, arching hips, trying to move closer to his mouth. "Please," she panted. "Please..." Charles' eyes locked with hers, and he gave her a tender smile. Then he covered her clitoris with his mouth. A shiver coursed through her, as he licked that nub of flesh; agonizingly slow at first, and then faster. He inserted another finger inside her, and she grasped his hair, her chest heaving. Just as her thighs began to shake, he moved away from her clitoris, making her whine. Charles then used his tongue to explore it, delving as deep as he could. She heard him moan in pleasure and realised he enjoyed this foreplay just as much as she did.

When, at last, they had satisfied all their desires, they lay back on the pillows, utterly spent, but still locked in each other's arms. Today culminated every one of their heart's desires and they fell into a deep slumber. They were awakened by the cock crowing daylight, and Charles wiped the sleep from his eyes and gently shook Charlotte from her slumber. They gazed into each other's eyes, with the affirmation that what had transpired last night was a glimpse of what their future held for them.

As the dawn was breaking, they quickly dressed and, with their valises in hand, headed to the stables to advise the driver they were ready for their journey north.

17

Once on board the coach, they found themselves in the company of three other passengers, a husband and wife and a gentleman, who happened to be in the tobacco trade. After all the introductions were made, the two women immediately struck up a conversation, exchanging stories as the men got to know each other. This was a Godsend, as it helped to make the long journey easier to bear. Charles learned a lot by talking with Mr. Isaac Reuben, who happened to be a tobacco trader and was informed of how this type of business could be quite profitable. He also learned that most of the trade was done in the city of Glasgow and was now the main centre for the importing and exporting of many different goods. It was a most jovial journey that they all shared, even though there were lots of hardships along the way, stopping at different Inns to change horses and have a sparse meal, before journeying on.

At long last, they crossed the border just as dawn was breaking, causing the hills and mountains to awaken from their slumber, to cast a myriad of colours in a welcoming fashion, for a long lost son. As they arrived in Glasgow, the tobacco trader told Charles to think of what they had spoken of, assuring Charles if he ever ventured back to Glasgow, to call on him. After saying their goodbyes, they all went their separate ways.

18

Now it was on to Edinburgh, where Charles couldn't wait to introduce his bride-to-be to his parents. Early the next morning, they stood outside his parents' door. The clatter of the horses' hooves reverberated on the cobblestones, awakening the sleeping household. His parents were unaware of Charles' accident, his hospitalization and the fact that he was heading home to them. So, to their utter amazement, when Calum and Megan, opened the front door, they saw this tall young man being helped from the carriage by a slip of a girl holding onto him for dear life. Calum quickly ran to the young couple, relieving the weight of Charlotte's charge onto his broad shoulders. "My God, Son, what has happened to you?" Megan, the organizing type of person, rebuked Calum, saying, "Bring them both into the front room and we will start asking questions then." As the four adults quietly shuffled through the doorway, Megan bit her lips to stop the tears of joy spilling down her face. Her beloved son was home, but at what cost? Calum took their luggage from the hallway and placed it in the spare room, before hurrying back to give the young couple a proper welcome. He thought it odd that his wife wasn't there, so when he found Megan in the scullery wiping her eyes with her apron, he reached out and gathered her into his arms, gently asking "What has happened, Dearest?" With a quiet sob, she answered him, "Charles has been gravely injured and

56

requires the best Scottish surgeons to take care of his knee, otherwise, he will lose his leg. That is why he has come home. He also told me that Charlotte, a nurse who has taken such good care of him, accompanied him on his journey here. Calum, they are in love and want our blessing." Assessing the situation very quickly, Calum told Megan, "Wipe those tears, my Love, do not let Charles know of your distress, we will take care of them both and put their minds at rest."

Composing themselves, they entered the sitting room, where Charles was resting comfortably with his shattered leg resting on three pillows piled high, giving him much relief. Calum walked over to Charles, extending his hand and welcomed his beloved son back home. He then gruffly asked Charles, "And who is this beautiful creature who has accompanied you?" Hearing his father's warm, welcoming voice. Charles said, "Father and Mother, this is Charlotte, my betrothed. She has been instrumental in my recovery and elected to assist me in my journey back to you both. We intend to wed in the old Kirk where Mother and you tied the knot. Charles' mother couldn't contain her excitement at this wonderful news and began telling Charlotte about the Church and all about her wedding day. "Megan," interrupted Calum "we have all the time in the world to get re-acquainted, so I think we should let this young couple rest for a while. Perhaps you can make some breakfast later and then we shall sit down and discuss what has to be done." At this statement from Calum, a surreal calmness befell on all of them. Charles knew his father would do his utmost to carry out their decisions for their wedding as best he could.

When they had finished eating, Charles asked about his beloved grandfather, and why he was absent from the homecoming. Megan and Calum's eyes met across the table, which did not go unnoticed by Charles. "Is something amiss, father?" he asked. Calum, clearing his throat, said, "Grandfather John peacefully passed away three years ago, and we were unable to contact you. But, rest assured, he died a happy and quiet death, knowing you had fulfilled your dream of becoming a major force in the King's Navy."

Charles sucked in his breath; it was as if he had been kicked in his stomach. He rose as quickly as he could, his chair clattering against the wall of the scullery, and asked to be excused. Hobbling into his old bedroom, which had been occupied by his beloved grandfather while he was at sea, he slumped down on the bed, his head throbbing from knowing that he would never see his grandfather again. Resting his elbows on his knees and holding his head in his hands, he felt the tears sting the back of his eyes and the sobs being stifled in his chest. He slowly lay down on the pillows, smelling that familiar smell of pipe tobacco that grandfather John smoked when the day's chores were finished and he had retired to his room. Then the memories came flooding back to Charles of all that grandfather John had shared and taught him. It was through this kindly man that he had grown to love fishing, finding treasures on the shore, and the love for the sea grew in him. Now, these memories would be imbedded into Charles' brain forever, knowing this wonderful man, his grandfather, was no more. It was both a good and a bad day for him, being reunited with his mother and father, introducing Charlotte to them, then the shattering news of the death of Grandfather John. Drying his eyes, he knew that he had to take this news in his stride, as this was the circle of life, and how we all must leave what we cherish.

After a few minutes, and composing himself as best he could, he returned downstairs to the family and apologised for his behaviour. His father knew how he must have been hurting inside, so, to lighten the mood he asked Charles and Charlotte if they had decided a date for their wedding. "As soon as possible, "Charles replied, moving his hand across the table to clasp Charlotte's hand in his. "Well tomorrow is as good a time as any," his Mother smiled. "Mr. Watt, the Meenster, shall be christening a new babby at 10 o'clock, so there's your opportunity to get things moving."

The next morning, they approached the minister after the christening and arranged to be married the following week. As Charles was still recuperating, and with no home to call their own, his father suggested they could stay with them, or live in the cottage until they got their affairs in order. "Thank you father, I'm sure the cottage would suit us fine and we're most grateful."

The wedding was a quiet affair, but even so, Charlotte looked radiant and she blushed when Charles told her how beautiful she was. His mother and father were witnesses to the happy event and, after the ceremony they walked the short distance to his parents' house. Charlotte was so happy, she felt as though she was floating on air, they spent a few hours at his parents' home, before making their way to the cottage.

Upon entering the cottage, Charlotte knew she would grow to love this little house. Charles took her on a small tour of the cottage, showing her his room when he stayed there with his grandfather and the old wooden bench at the back of the cottage, where he used to sit listening to old John's stories about the animals and birds of the forest. Charlotte took his hand saying "You really miss him, don't you?" "Of course I do, but you are my life and first concern now and the past must be laid to rest, but never forgotten."

Charles lit the fire in the old ingle nook and sat on the chair that old John used, causing the happy memories to return as he watched the flames flicker in the fireplace, which added to a cosy glow that came from the storm lights which were causing a lived-in ambience to the cottage. Charlotte filled a large pot and placed it on the stove intending to tidy up, as the cottage had gathered dust and some cobwebs after lying empty for quite a while. As she was about to move away, Charles grasped her elbow and pulled her down onto his knee, before placing her face between his hands and kissing her passionately. "You have beauty that is beyond compare," he whispered into her ear, as his hand fondled her breast. "This was my lovely day and I shall carry it in my memory forever," she sighed, placing her hand on his, the one that was caressing her breast.

Upon hearing this, Charles rose from his chair, clasped her hand and guided her into the bedroom, where he let all his sexual emotions run free, as he gently lowered her onto the bed. She felt slightly cold when he removed her gown, but the warmth quickly returned when he began kissing her neck, before teasing each nipple of her firm breasts, making them come erect, as he tugged and sucked them with his lips. She gasped as he slid his hand up her inner thigh as he searched for her hidden treasure. Charlotte could not resist to what she was feeling and surrendered herself up to him, as he began kissing her breasts once more. Now she felt a need that was so new to her, she wanted him inside her and shuddered when she felt his arousal throb against her leg. Now she wanted more than being kissed, she moved her hand down his belly, until she felt the thick pubic hair, then carried on until she grasped his shaft and slid it against her open labia. She seemed to spasm as he lowered his body between her legs and heard herself cry out as he plunged his length into her. She cried out once more as he gripped her hips and drove deeper still, until she thought his shaft was about to touch her heart. Charlotte felt on fire, as Charles drove into her with such ferocity, before calling out her name as he emptied himself inside of her. Charles knew, by the way she was shivering with pleasure, she wanted more, so he traced his tongue down her body, moving his tongue to between her thighs to tease her and moving in rhythm with the slow thrusts of her hips towards his mouth. Suddenly, he felt her arching her back and let out a low moan as the floodgates opened and her love juices trickled down her thigh. As Charles moved away, she hated the feeling that he had taken all his love with him, but when he returned with a damp cloth to wash both their bodies, her world was back on its axis, as he lay down beside her and rested his head on her breast, slowly stroking her soft body until sleep overtook them.

The following weeks were the perfect cure for Charles, he was growing stronger by the day, with Charlotte being his inspiration, and their love knew no bounds. He kept himself busy by helping at his father's shop, but he knew what he wanted and that was to be his own man.

19

Over the coming weeks, Charles pondered the type of business that would be suitable for him, as he realised manual work was out of the question, due to his disability. Then, one night, a thought suddenly struck him, why not contact Mr. Isaac Rueben, the gentleman he met on the coach, and find out the procedure for entering the import and exporting of foreign goods? He discussed his plan with Charlotte and she was quite happy and willing to go along with his plan.

The following week, Charles set out for Glasgow and, upon arriving quite late, he took a small room at one of the city's Inns. Early the next morning, he made his way to the address of the building where

Mr. Isaacs conducted his business. After stating his reason for being there, a young clerk took him to the office where Mr. Reuben sat with his head buried in a ledger. The moment he saw Charles, he rose and shook him warmly by the hand. "It's wonderful to see you again young man, what brings you to Glasgow, but more to the point, how is life treating you, well I hope?" "I really can't complain," answered Charles "but, as you know, I was at sea from a very young age and have no other experience of anything, other than the Navy and what I know is all about shipping, I was looking to you for some advice on importing and exporting goods," "I'll be only too glad to help you Charles, but my first piece of advice is, if you pursue this line of business, do so in Edinburgh, as there are too many people here in the city earning their living at this trade. I take it you won't be travelling home tonight, so I would like to offer you some hospitality and you can stay at my home for a few nights and I can give you an insight of what the work entails."

Charles knew he couldn't refuse such an offer and the next day he wrote to Charlotte what had taken place. Isaac had a beautiful four roomed house in Binnie Place and this area was where most of the influential traders lived. Over the next few days, Charles was made most welcome by Isaac's family who treated him as one of their own and, in his spare time, he gleaned all the information that was kindly given to him. However, his biggest surprise was yet to come, for on the morning he was about to say his farewells, Isaac walked with him to the coach that would take him back home. Just as he was about to enter the coach, Isaac informed him that he was going to retire shortly, and gave him a short list of the firms that he had dealt with over the years and told him to keep in touch and let him know how he was progressing. Charles was stuck for words at this wonderful gesture, but the look on his face must have shown Isaac how grateful he was. "I can only thank you from the bottom of my heart and I shall never forget your kindness shown to me." "Just stay healthy and have a long and prosperous life, you deserve it and give my regards to your Lady wife," Isaac replied as they shook hands warmly.

As the coach moved off, Charles looked back and knew he had met a true gentleman. Arriving back at Edinburgh, he couldn't get home fast enough to share his good news. That evening, he laid out his plans to Charlotte and the more he explained his intentions, the more excited she became at the thought of her Charles becoming a successful businessman.

20

A few weeks later, he rented a small office in the centre of town and, being new to this type of work, trading was slow, but with his good business acumen, he was soon importing goods from all over the continent, mostly from the people that Isaac had traded with. He began by importing flax from St. Helena's, wines and brandy from France and, as he was doing this, he was exporting meat, whisky and tartan cloth that was being woven in the Highland crofts. Within a year, his business was booming, to the point that he had to employ seven workers to cope with the influx of goods, and there was no sign of it slowing down. Fortune was smiling down on both Charles and Charlotte, but the best was yet to come.

One night, as they sat by the cosy glow from the fire, he noticed that Charlotte appeared to be lost in thought as she sat with pen in hand at their small writing bureau. "A penny for them," he asked, rising from his chair before laying his hands on her shoulders and kissing her neck. Charlotte quickly covered what she had been writing with her hand, saying, "Just bide your time, Charles, you'll soon have your answer." When she had finished writing a short while later, she handed the piece of paper to Charles saying, "I want you to decide, my love." He was taken aback at what she had said, but the moment he saw what she had written, made his heart skip a beat, the sheet of paper was full of names for boys and girls. "Charlotte my dearest, what a beautiful surprise, I never thought for a moment that…" before he could say another word, she rushed into his arms, hugging him as she asked "Are you truly happy my dear?" "Lassie, no man will ever be blessed with the happiness that you have given me this night, you have made my life complete."

A baby girl was born later in the year and they named her Claire, then two years later they were blessed with a boy, whom they named Ewan. Like his father before him, Ewan grew into a fine young man, but unlike his father, he was quite happy to work in the family business, making it prosper and grow to the extent that they needed larger warehouses.

At the age of 28, Ewan was introduced to the daughter of one of his business associates and it was love at first sight. They wed two years later and she was given the 'Topaz Butterfly' as a token of his love and devotion to her, and on their wedding night, she sat in wonder and realised how special she now had become, as he told her the story of how the brooch had been handed down lovingly through the ages.

As the years passed, they became caring and loving parents to three daughters, Fiona, Lorna and Eliza and their last born was a boy whom they named Angus. So, it was now up to this boy to carry on the chain of events that began with Calum, when he originally crafted the 'Topaz Butterfly'.

Over the coming years, Angus entered the same line of work as his father, starting as a clerk and, eventually, through hard work and study, he became a partner in his Father's flourishing export trade and through his expertise became a prolific businessman, before marrying and keeping the family tradition alive.

Over the coming years, the Topaz Butterfly was religiously handed down from husband to wife and then, from mother to son, who would knowingly continue the aged old custom of presenting it to his bride on their wedding day.

The business and the Butterfly were both destined to be eventually handed down to my father, John, from my grandfather. At the beginning of the great war of 1914 -18, at the young age of 17, John enlisted with the Royal Scots, which was an old Highland regiment and he was so proud to become the company bugler. He saw action on the French battlefield of Ypres but, unfortunately, three weeks before hostilities ended, he was injured in a gas attack which left him with a damaged lung, thus hindering his breathing for the rest of his life.

After taking a long overdue rest and recuperating for a few months, he returned to the company, to find that, because of the war the business had floundered for a long period. Over a few weeks, the trading began picking up once more as some of the workers who had gone off to war returned to make the business flourish once more. Sadly, a few of the original staff lost their lives in the war but, when his grandfather was informed of some of the widows' predicaments of putting bread on the table for their families, his generosity shone through, by giving each of the wives a small amount of money at the end of each month to help them overcome their burden. Now that my father felt stronger, he used all his business acumen and contacts making the business thrive and grow once more, leaving him no option but to get more storage space. He discussed a plan with his father that he would like to move to Glasgow and open a new branch there and be successful in his own right. His father agreed to this idea, as he wanted his son to become independent and be his own man. Having been successful in acquiring a good size workplace, he, along with his small staff, worked hard to make the business prosper. He kept in touch with his father who gave him a better insight to gaining new imports from other new customers and, within a year, he had purchased a small house and hired a maid to keep the place in order, as most of his leisure time was taken up with the business. He felt he had to get out more and pursue his favourite hobby of going fly fishing in some country lochs and rivers.

One Saturday night, he was coerced by some his workers to go along to a local dance that was to be held in the Highlanders Institute. This hall was to become the meeting place for many of the folk who had come down to Glasgow, from the North and many of them came from the Highlands and islands where most of them spoke the Gaelic. This was the night that my father met this beautiful girl, Martha McGregor, who was born and raised on the island of Barra. She and two of her friends had come down to the city to find employment. As work was scarce in their village, my father told me, much later, that she was advised to attend these dances where she would meet some of her fellow Highlanders and she would then be in the company of her own people.

When my older sister became inquisitive to ask my mother how she met and married my father, she was told that my father looked every inch the gentleman when he approached her and asked her to dance and, after a few dances, she hoped that he would like to see her again. Her hopes came to fruition and, after a two-year courtship; they married in the year 1921. Over the coming years they were blessed with two daughters, Fiona and Marie. With the import business booming, the family had a very comfortable lifestyle, but that all changed in late 1929, when the business began to falter.

23

Within the last months of 1929, the country found itself in a state of chaos. A colossal depression originated in the U.S.A. and quickly spread throughout the world. Thankfully, the British depression was not as severe as the other countries, i.e. Germany, Canada and even Australia. The British unemployed reached the staggering figure of 3.5 million, causing every family in the land hardship that they had never known. The effect of this depression was devastating, there was a food shortage and, when the butcher shops, or grocery stores had any stock, people who hadn't the money to purchase what was on offer, the best they could do, was to seek out the men who dealt on the Black Market.

These men could always find a way of getting their hands on what you needed, at a lower cost. As the demand for British products collapsed, most factories and business companies closed, including my father's and my grandfather's. I imagine it must have been a sad day for them when they had to lay off their staff, knowing it would be nigh impossible for them to obtain other employment. He also came to realise that the upkeep of the large house, in which the family lived, had now become a burden and the only viable solution was to sell it and look for smaller accommodation. The house was eventually sold off at a much-underrated value and the family moved to smaller rented accommodation in the East end of the City. The money that they received from selling the house, helped tide them over until my father found office work in a bakery company, where he stayed until the outbreak of World War II. Although he was now 39, he tried to re-enlist, but wasn't accepted. His lungs were too badly damaged, so he got a new job at a carpet factory which was now producing hoses for the war effort. I was born in 1941 'a war baby' so to speak.

24

Now that the war was finally over, I must have been about 4 years of age, but I still remember the large bonfire in the middle of the street and the neighbours dancing into the wee small hours. I can also remember my two sisters, who were working at a munition's factory in Coventry, arriving at the door to be met by my tearful mother and hugged by my father. They hadn't seen my sisters for over two years, so it was a happy homecoming, which lasted long into the night, as they regaled all that happened in the past few years.

This was a wonderful time for me and, looking back, I now realise I was spoiled and most weekends were spent with one of my sisters, who would often take me into the large stores in the City and buy me a comic book or, for a special treat, take me to the cinema. Everything was rationed and, with money being scarce, most nights were spent at home playing games like snakes and ladders, or I would join my father in his pigeon loft, filling the tiny seed boxes, or the small water bowls, while the birds would give their soft cooing noise and appeared to be nodding their heads in approval.

I also remember the fun weekends that I would spend playing football with my pals in the street, until it was late and time for bed. These happy nights ended when I was told I would be starting school the following week. This is something I hadn't bargained for, and all sorts of terrible thoughts ran riot in my head but, in the end, being promised some sweets for being a brave boy, helped to sway me.

I remember that morning well, as I had never seen so many children howling and crying, as their escorts left them in the classroom with this strange woman. Through my young eyes, while fighting to keep my own scared tears from falling, she appeared very old. If memory serves correct, her name was Miss Heafey and, another thing that springs to mind, was that once some semblance of order was restored, we were told we would get to sit on the large black rocking horse which stood in the corner of the classroom. The teacher then formed a line and, one by one, we were lifted onto the horse. I was about eighth in line and when I was helped onto the horse, I felt the seat of my trousers grow wet. The girl, who was on the horse before me, had an accident, so we both suffered from wet pants. Needless to say, the horse riding was put off for another day until the saddle was dry.

School was alright, I was always attentive and eager to learn what was being taught but, I was more interested in getting home to play football in the street with my pals. This all changed though, when I reached the age of 7 and found myself in Mr. Jim Gillespie's class. The way in which he taught, made me sit up and take notice, as he made learning fun and interesting by the manner in how he would explain things. I believe he and another lady teacher, Miss Malone, who would be the next tutor to teach our next class, were the two people who gave me a zest for learning. Around this time, my young sister Anne, who was now five years of age, was enrolled in my school, so that meant my mother would come and collect her every day, as she left school earlier than I did.

When she was six, Anne began to leave her class at 4 o'clock, the same time as I did, but my Mother still came down to meet her, so we would all walk home together. Before then, I would rush home, get changed into my old clothes and go out to play, now I sauntered along in the background, as I thought that if any of my pals saw me with my mother, it would look as though I was being collected from school.

Over the coming weeks a girl named Alexis, who was in my class and sat at the desk in front of me, had also started walking with us, as we were both around eight years of age, but I never gave it a second thought. She lived in the next street to ours and, on the way home, she would hold my sister's hand while chatting away to my mother, until she came to her street, and then she would leave us.   Alexis sat at a few desks in front of me and was always first to finish whatever we were told to do. She was so clever and quite happy to help, if you were finding things difficult, and it wasn't the first time she assisted me with a problem that I would be I would be having. She had such a grown up outlook and always had a captivating smile. The one and only time I ever saw her sad and without that smile, was the week before Christmas. I returned to class after leaving the playground and found Alexis sitting sobbing at her desk, when I asked her what was wrong, she told me one of the boys in our class told her there was no Santa Claus, this really upset her, but Mr Gillespie, who had also noticed her crying sat beside her at the desk and he must have explained to her that our parents had taken over the role of Santa. Over the coming weeks, I began walking beside her and listened to what Alexis and my mother spoke about, and it was mostly about her mother and her brother and sisters, and that to me was completely boring, couldn't they talk about something else, anything for a change.

One Monday, Alexis wasn't at her desk, which was unusual, as she was never absent from class, she didn't show up for the rest of the week and it felt kind of strange that she wasn't there to walk home beside my mother who, when asked, said she may have had to stay at home if she was ill, and not fit enough for school, As she didn't attend class for another week, I approached Mr. Gillespie to inquire if he knew the reason Alexis wasn't coming to school and he told me that her family had moved to England.

When I explained this to my mother, she said she was sorry to hear this, as she had grown so fond of Alexis. Now there were other things to think about, I had reached the age of 7 and that meant preparing to make my first Holy Communion, which is an important part of any Catholic's life. I wasn't looking forward to this, as it's all about getting dressed up in a silk shirt, wearing a red sash and being fussed over, before being warned to be on my best behaviour. To be honest, all I remember was, after the Mass, I was going with my big sister to get my photograph taken on this special day, it might have been for them, but it couldn't end quick enough for me as I wanted to get rid of the fancy clothes and into my old togs.

The rest of the year was uneventful, that is until the day I turned 8, and went to join the local Library. Over the coming weeks, football after school, was forgotten about as I was now lost in a world of my own, as I browsed amongst the books. I would imagine what it would be like to be with Jim Hawkins on the Hispaniola, or out on the rough seas with a whaling boat listening to Captain Ahab screaming out orders as we chased the white whale, known to the crew as Moby Dick. This was my doorway to a world of fantasy and adventure, as it took me away from the ordinary uneventful days. The library is where I learned much about life. I could sit at one of the tables and be transported to every corner of the world, getting to know how other people in other different countries lived. I would often eavesdrop on a conversation between some of the older men, who always seemed to be there, no matter what time I showed up. I soon realised that most of them were out of work, or retired, but they all had one thing in common, they all seemed to be very intelligent and what they had gleamed mostly came from being avid readers.

As I couldn't afford to buy comics, I would always get a book to read over the weekend. So, on the Friday after I left school, my first stop would be the library, before making my way home. Going through the old worn swing doors, I would be in my comfort zone, as I noticed some of the usual faces who were always seemed to be there, reading the daily newspapers that the library supplied, or their head buried in a book. There were two old men in particular whom I loved to see. They always seemed to have different views, and it would get to the stage where the conversation became heated and loud. It never bothered me, but what I found hilarious, was the librarian, who was a very stern looking woman, would lower her head, peer over the wire rimmed pince-nez spectacles, which were balanced on the very end of her nose, before literally bellowing in a loud voice, "SILENCE", I don't think she realised that she was making more noise than anyone in the room.

On one of my regular after school visits, I was making for the adventure section, when I heard a soft voice saying "Martin? "As I turned around, I noticed Alexis sitting at one of the tables, she looked up and smiled, "I thought it was you, but I didn't picture you as a bookworm," she said in a low voice. "I'm not. I'm just in here to get out of the cold and to see if they have any books with pictures, what are you reading by the way?" "Anne of Green Gables, it's a book for girls. Oh no! I didn't realise what time it was, I'd better be going." "Hold on a minute, while I pick a book and we can walk home together," I said. "Alright, but hurry, I'm late as it is." I picked up the closest book at hand and off we went.

I saw a different side to Alexis that day, in a way she had changed. I found that she had a wicked sense of humour to go with her grown up outlook. We laughed a lot on the way home and that broke the ice, as we found we had much in common. Now that she was back in my class once more, we began walking home together again after school, with me telling her mostly about things that had taken place at school, while she was away, and her telling me how she missed all her friends and how glad she was to be back home, as she wasn't happy living in England.

As money was scarce, the next few years were boring; everything seemed to be the same, month after month, with nothing to look forward to, apart from the weekends. That's when you went to the children's movie matinee on a Saturday. Even then, I sometimes missed that, due to the lack of a few pennies, but I would still go to the library with Alexis each Friday, as that broke the monotony, plus the good thing was, it didn't cost any money.

This was the year that Alexis and I ended attending our primary school and, after the summer holidays, would be enrolling in the senior secondary school. This was also the year that, because of the workload of intense studying which we both had to do, we seemed to see less and less of each other, until it came to the point, when she went out of my life completely. To be quite candid, the Academy was just a holding pattern for me, where I circled aimlessly, until I could leave, get a job and earn some money to help my mother cope financially.

25

Even though it would be a meagre amount, the extra money would help financially, in some small way. Now I was about to find out for myself that the happiest days of your life were really spent at school. Much to my chagrin, that well- known saying really struck home when I got my first job in the local leather factory. My task was to roll up cowhides that had been shorn of their hair, lift them onto my shoulder and carry them to a lime pit where they would soak until they became pliable. As I was small of stature and weighed less than the hide, it seemed a wonderful way to get a hernia for the princely sum of 14 shillings a week I lasted a fortnight before giving up in defeat, mainly due to the fact I was beginning to walk lop-sided with one shoulder lower than the other. I felt if I had continued working there, I'm sure my knuckles would have been dragging along the ground.

The following week I was fortunate enough to get a job with J.R. Moore and Son, a plumbing and electrical heating company and, for the first few months, I was the "gofer" it was go for this, or go for that, but that all ended, when I began my apprenticeship as a plumber and heating engineer. Now here was a job I could really get my interested in. I was learning something new every day, as the men you were assigned to, always gave you the chance to be "hands-on" as they watched over you. I had a great rapport with the rest of the tradesmen and, the most interesting part of the day, was at lunch time, when the men, who were football fans, would argue about all sorts of things and many a referee's ears must have been red hot.

I found it strange that there was one man who always sat alone at the corner of the workbench reading. I had never worked with him, until one day the foreman said to me, "You'll be working with Scoop this morning and he'll show you how to wire up the dynamo in that new heater." My curiosity got the better of me and I just had to ask, "Why do they call him Scoop?" His name is Harry Blair, and as far as I've been told, he was nick-named after a photographer who wrote for the local paper and was known as "Scoop Bell". He was a freelance photographic journalist and covered all types of human-interest stories, mostly car crashes and any other sort of daily mishaps that took place. It wouldn't be my way to earn a living, but I suppose somebody has got to keep us informed about this sort of thing. Hearing this, struck a note in me, as I imagined how it must be to show up at the scene and report first-hand the outcome of what had taken place, then take photos and give the readers an insight into the cause and the aftermath of the accident.

As it so happened, I always had, among other things, a faint curiosity in cameras and would have liked to know more about how they produced photographs and now the answer was walking towards me. "I'm Jackie and you'll be working wi' me oan a dynamo and then we've some o' the new tenement hooses doon the Gallowgate that's tae get new heaters fitted, so get the gear an' we'll make a start. Whit dae we ca' you by the way?" "Well, it's no by the way, to begin with, an' you can ca' me Martin." He laughed at my response, stuck out his hand and said "Ah'm Harry, pleased tae meet ye' son, ah like a man wi' a sense o'humour." That was the beginning of a long friendship which lasted over the years.

My interest in taking pictures really took hold when I found myself sitting next to him at the tea break one afternoon. I asked him how he got involved in photography. He told me that when he was much younger, every weekend would find him outdoors, fishing or hill climbing and on getting back home, he would think of all the wonderful scenery that he had witnessed and how the clouds could suddenly change all the colours of the landscape and the terrain in the blink of an eye. He said that coming back home, after one of the days out on the hill; he thought it would be great to capture all these wonderful things that the countryside had to offer. Then he would be able to look back and recall these special moments. He realised the answer was to buy a camera. So he bought one, and he's been taking photos ever since. The next day, he brought in some of his photos and, I must admit, on seeing these fantastic pictures I was left speechless.

Harry wasn't only a first-class plumber; he was also an artist, in his own special way. He told me that every now and then he would submit some of his work to newspapers, or country magazines, and if they got printed in any of the magazines, he received a cheque for a few pounds and that helped him buy better equipment. I was hooked. I wanted to know everything about how to begin taking photographs and Harry was only too willing to give me advice on getting started. He told me to purchase an inexpensive camera, just in case the notion wore off.

Then, after a couple of weeks went by, he took me to his camera club and began by teaching me how to develop my own reels of film and how to set up and focus the enlarger. I felt right at home here and began coming to the club at every chance I got. On Harry's advice I bought a fairly new second-hand camera and now, looking back, I must admit my young sister and my pals, got to the stage they were getting fed up with getting my camera shoved in their face, but they soon changed their tune when they were handed their photo.

A few years went by and I was becoming more proficient with the camera and sometimes Harry would ask me to the occasional wedding, where he was the official photographer and I would often help him set up the camera lighting. But, more importantly; I got the chance to watch Harry at work, gleaning how he would compose the wedding party to take shots of them at different angles and at different backgrounds. This is how I picked up lots of useful tips, which came in handy over the coming years. But, for the moment, I was leading a very busy life between working during the day and going to the camera club at night.

26

It so happened, while I was on my way to the camera club one Friday night and, little did I know, that this was the night that would change my life. Just as I left the house and into the street, who should be walking towards me, but Pat Cairney, one of my pals whom I hadn't seen over the past few weeks. "Where have you been hiding, we all thought you had croaked it?" Pat was what you would call a loveable rogue, but great fun to be with. "How's thing? How are ye gettin' oan?" "Pat, ah cannae get oan fer falllin' aff," I replied, "It's work, work, work just now, we're really busy installin' heaters in some high-rise flats that's just been built, ah've hardly got a minute tae myself." "Ah know whit you neeed boyo, and that's tae come wi' the rest o' the boys tae wee Peter McCabe's birthday party on Saturday night. His family huv moved up tae that new housing scheme ca'ed Cranhill, but before we go tae the party, we're goin' tae a dance in the community hall, an' if we're lucky, dig up a few lassies tae go wi'us." "Ah don't feel up tae it Pat, ah was planning a quiet night in, ah'm really tired an' ah'm working on Sunday." "C'mon, ye owe yersel' a night oot wi' the boys, ye know it makes sense." He's right, I thought, that's exactly what I need. "O.K. whit's the plan?" I asked. "We're aw' meeting at hauf past seven, then gettin' the bus tae Cranhill fer the hoot 'n' Annie, then oan tae the party.

Saturday found me on my way to the local baths to have a shower to try and get myself in the mood for the coming party. But even that didn't help, as I still felt reluctant to go to this party. However, as I told Pat I would meet them, I had to stick to my word. After supper, I was feeling apprehensive and, in a way, I wished I hadn't made these arrangements with Pat. However, after leaving the house to meet the boys, I felt much better and was happy that I agreed to meet them. We all met as planned and made our way to Cranhill and stopped off at the old Community Hall where the dance was being held. Approaching the hall, the party seemed to be in full swing, as we could hear the music coming from the loud speakers in the hall and the cacophony of music and laughter seemed to add to the party mood. Following behind a few girls, who were walking through the door of the hall, Pat's remarks to us were, "Right lads, every man for himself." Once inside, it took a while to get accustomed to the darkness, as the only light came from a mirrored ball hanging from the ceiling, giving everyone the appearance of a silver spotted Dalmatian dog, as our clothes were covered in white spots emanating from the revolving mirrors on the twirling ball.

Some of the boys got up to dance, leaving Pat and me on our own. Now that my eyes were becoming accustomed to the darkness, I began to study some of the girls in a faraway corner of the hall. I noticed there was something familiar about one girl in particular, but I just couldn't put my finger on it, as I couldn't remember where I had seen her before. Pat followed my gaze and told me, "You had better forget that one. I bet her boyfriend is hanging around somewhere." It was only when she turned around, did I realize who she was. Was this the girl I once knew from grammar school, and there was only one way to satisfy my curiosity. So, right away, I turned to Pat and said, "I'm going to dance with her." "In yer dreams, matey, you don't have a snowball's chance in hell," was his put-down reply. Winding my way along the side of the dance hall, I stood watching for a moment, while she was finishing her conversation with her friend, before making my move.

Touching her elbow, I spoke softly into her ear, "Do you still believe in Santa Claus?" Turning her head towards me, she gasped "Martin, is it really you? You remembered me after all this time." "How could I possibly forget the wee girl who walked home from school, holding my Mother's hand every day?" Her smile lit up her face, as the memories of that time resurfaced. I took her hand while leading her onto the dance floor and said, "Let's remember those times together." Holding her close, while dancing to a slow ballad, and, as we passed by Pat, I looked over Alexis's shoulder; I gave him a wink and a big grin. Upon seeing this, he shook his head, looking at the floor as if to say, "I don't believe it." Coming off the floor, we stood at the soft-drinks bar, regaling the past few years. Just then, her friend came over and said they were ready to leave for the party.

"That wouldn't happen to be Peter McCabe's party, would it?" "As a matter of fact, it is," Alexis replied. "But to be honest, I didn't want to go, but I didn't want to let my friends down." "Now here's the rub, I felt the same way," was my response, "but, like you, I too was coerced into going. So, let's say we get our coats and make for the door?" "Now there's an idea." she replied, "we can catch up on some of the past."

The next few hours were spent reminiscing, and all the old memories came flooding back, getting to know how our lives had fared since we had last been together as school friends. The more we talked, the more I became enamoured by her outgoing personality and warmth. In the short time that we were together, I felt myself becoming attracted to her. I had never felt this way before, and this was something new to me, having a girl with a tremendous outlook on life and a wicked sense of humour. In no time at all, we were standing at the entranceway to her home and I don't know what possessed me, but suddenly, I pulled her into my arms, and to my surprise, she didn't resist, as our lips blended in an all-consuming way. "Wow," she said breathlessly, "that was something I certainly wasn't expecting, but it was wonderful!" I couldn't find the words to reply to her, as I searched for the words to express how I felt. Suddenly, the spell was broken by the noise of an upstairs door slamming. As I said goodnight and began walking away, I could hear her fumbling with her house keys to unlock her door, and, at that very same moment, unlocked the doubt I was harbouring of being rejected by asking her out again. As I was about to make my way back to the old dance hall to meet my friends, I turned around and, as I did, as if on cue, she looked over her shoulder and gave me that enchanting smile and that was all I needed to rush towards her and take her into my arms once more.   Those few hours seemed to have changed my life forever, as we began seeing each other two or three times a week. Since I had first met Alexis, the hours I spent at work seemed to pass ever so slowly, especially if we had made any plans to be together, I was becoming the proverbial clock watcher, counting the minutes to be with her.

27

The next two years seemed to fly past, we enjoyed many wonderful times, but, there would be the occasional interruption of meaningless quarrels, mostly caused by my youthful frustrations, from hormones which seemed to spiral out of control, but I could understand the reason for her rejection of these youthful urges. However, that did not assuage my need for her. I remember one night, as we stood petting, I tried to explain how I needed some relief by saying that if I went into a shop and asked for a certain brand of cigarettes and they had none, I would probably shop somewhere else. Her reply to that was, "I think you had better give up smoking then." God, I certainly loved that girl's sense of humour!

Within the following couple of weeks, I would turn 21 and my apprenticeship would come to an end, making me a fully-fledged Heating Engineer. The only problem being, I was now expected to travel throughout the country on special working assignments. That meant leaving Alexis on her own, giving her a chance to spend more time with her friends, most of whom were her college colleagues. I didn't relish the thought of having to travel, as that would mean long stretches of being away from Alexis, but as this was part of the conditions of my job, I just had to grin and bear it. As it so happened, my birthday would fall on a Friday and, unfortunately, I was asked by the foreman if I would like to travel to Hull with some of the older Engineers, on the following Monday, to install a complete heating system in a new shopping centre. I could have refused and let one of the other boys take my place, but as it was only for a few weeks, it meant that I would be on a better rate of pay and the extra money I earned could help my mother, as my young sister was now a shop assistant with very meagre wages and every little bit helped. That's when I then made up my mind to celebrate my birthday by having dinner with Alexis that night at Fellini's, a small Italian restaurant, which we visited regularly, before breaking the news to her about my next project.

Arrangements were made to meet at 7:00 pm, but, as luck would have it, Alexis seemed to have been delayed. As I sat there, nursing a small glass of wine, my eyes were constantly on the door, expecting Alexis to show up at any moment and, when she did, all eyes seemed to be upon her. As she walked through the door, she looked stunning wearing a red wool wrap around her shoulders, and when her wrap was slowly slipped off by Franco, it revealed her svelte figure, which was encased in a pencil slim short black dress which stopped short above her knees, adding to the aura that seemed to envelop her. As Franco escorted her to our table, I felt the envy of every man in the room. As she sat down, I sensed her excitement, as she seemed anxious to reveal something important. As she sat facing me, legs crossed, I couldn't tear my eyes away from them and began to imagine how it would feel to run my hand from her ankle, slowly up between her thighs, before plunging my fingers into her hidden treasure. I was captured, a prisoner of love by this sensuous, adorable girl. She reached under the table, and then placing her hand on my thigh, slowly stroked her fingers upwards. Looking into her eyes I whispered softly into her ear, "Whatever you are searching for, is not in there." She looked confused. "Oh, I am pretty sure I want this." She replied. "I'm sure you do, but there is something else for you in the inside pocket of my jacket."

She continued stroking my thigh, before removing her fingers from the top of my leg. She looked even more confused when I repeated, "What you're looking for is not in there." She sat for a moment simply staring at me, before I took her hand and moved it inside my left breast pocket of my jacket. Her curious stare transformed into one of complete surprise as she slowly retrieved the small velvet box that held the Topaz Butterfly brooch, which I had placed in my pocket. As she opened the box and gazed at the gift, her eyes lit up as she sat gazing at it, and then her tears began to fall. I raised my hand and gently wiped a tear from her cheek with my thumb, and quietly said, "This occasion does not call for tears, only happiness, as this brooch represents my love for you, and I want you to accept it place of an engagement ring." My heart seemed to register it, before my brain could process her answer. There was applause from all around us, as other patrons signalled their approval, as they watched Alexis wrapping her arms around my neck and kissing me deeply. I felt the wetness of her tears as our cheeks pressed together, as she repeated her answer in my ear, "Yes." There was no sense in finishing our meal, as we were too over-whelmed to eat. I paid the bill, left a generous tip and departed the restaurant to another round of applause.

As we made our way home, she wished me a happy birthday, before telling me what she had in store for my birthday gift. Seemingly, she had told her best friend, Kathleen, she was at a loss of what to get me for my birthday, when Kathleen responded by saying, "I have the very idea of the perfect gift for him, which would benefit both of you." Kathleen went on to say that her parents, who had a caravan down at the coast in Saltcoats, Ayrshire, were going out of town and wouldn't be returning until late Sunday night, and she also added, jokingly, "Don't do anything that I wouldn't do, and if so, be careful." That night Alexis told me about my birthday gift. When she told me this I was taken aback by her wonderful surprise. This was something I could only envisage in my wildest dreams, being alone with this beautiful girl, just being close to her, was all that I desired.

The only drawback was to let Alexis's mother know why she would not be home over the weekend. We both agreed that a small white lie would not go amiss by telling her mother that some of Alexis's friends were having a get together for a friend, who was about to be married, and they were all going to stay over at Kathleen's house.

Alexis and I agreed to meet on Saturday lunchtime at the train station. Then we would make our way to Kathleen's parents' beach house for the weekend. It seemed like hours had passed, as I sat in the waiting room at the train station, the first thing that came to mind was Alexis may have had second thoughts, but when she did arrive, she looked stunning. "Sorry I'm late, but I had to wait for Kathleen to give me the keys to her parents' caravan."   Now, the only problem I had was having to tell her I would be leaving early Monday morning, to travel to Hull, with some of the engineers to install heating equipment in a new school which was being built. This job would last around four weeks. On being told this, Alexis looked a bit forlorn, but realised this was part and parcel of my occupation. But, being Alexis, she wouldn't let her feelings spoil the evening and seemed to be more anxious to spend what little time we had together, without letting this spoil my birthday, and her surprise.

As we had never been in this part of the country, we had to stop and ask some strangers for directions to the caravan park and, as usually happens, most of the people we asked, said they were strangers to the district. Eventually, we found a lady who was kind enough to give us the accurate directions to where the caravan park was situated and, since she was going our way, she was kind enough to accompany us part of the way to our destination. After thanking this kind lady, we walked up the pathway and entered the caravan.

We had a brief tour, without being too intrusive, and then Alexis clasped my hand in hers before asking, "Well, what do you think?" "I think I've died and gone to Heaven; I never knew a caravan could be so large with all the mod cons," I replied. Alexis looked in the refrigerator and found that it was well-stocked, enough to last for a few days, and then she asked me if I felt like a bite to eat. "That is the furthest thing in my mind," I replied. "First things first, I am dying to try out that shower, and then get down to more important things." The look on Alexis's was one of mock surprise, leaving her to ponder what lay ahead.

Leaving Alexis in the lounge room, I undressed and stepped into the shower. After a few moments considering how to set this strange contraption in motion, the hot water eventually hit me with a sudden force. This was such a sublime feeling, having the water cascade against my body, like hot sharp needles. This feeling was something I could encounter every day of the week.

Just before turning off the water, I heard the bathroom door open, and through the steam on the shower door, I could see the silhouette of Alexis standing there with a large white towel wrapped around her body. "Would you like your birthday gift now?" she quietly asked, before releasing the towel, displaying her complete nakedness. She then stepped into the shower behind me. Wrapping her arms around me, I could feel her pressing her erect nipples against my back. Time seemed to stand still for me and, before I realised it, Alexis was enveloped in my arms. We stood under the spray for a moment rinsing off. I reached for the soap and covered her body with lather. As I kissed her passionately, I let my hand stray over her chest and down her stomach until I reached between her legs. This moment was all I envisioned it to be, our tongues were entwined in a teasing ritual dance, as my hands traced over her statuesque body, I placed one of her breasts in my mouth and I tormented her nipple with my tongue, causing her to gasp with pleasure. I began to fondle her mons, which was covered with soft downy pubic hairs. Slowly, but gently, placing my fingers into her love grotto, I could feel her body tremble as she felt the pressure of my fingers exploring her virgin vaginal walls. As one thing led to another, I gently parted her legs with my knee and, as she began to slide her hand along my throbbing shaft, we seemed to lose all our inhibitions and on turning her around she placed her hands on the tiled wall, allowing me to slowly enter her from behind. She uttered a gasp and urged me to push harder, as she moaned, "Oh my God!" I complied with her wishes and, as I thrust harder, her body seemed to stiffen as I tore through her hymen. I could feel her body shudder momentarily, and she let out a sharp cry. I asked her if I had hurt her, but she replied, "No darling, tonight I feel sensational. You have truly made me a woman and I shall always be yours." Sinking to the floor, feeling completed sated, I watched as Alexis etched on the steam covered glass, a heart with an arrow through it, saying 'A loves M' just as lovers, in the past, had done in bygone years. This said it all for me. After we towelled each other dry, we proceeded into the kitchen where Alexis prepared a small salad for a meal for both of us.

After finishing our light meal, we proceeded to the bedroom to rest for a little while. Again, my body seemed to overwhelm me with the emotions I felt for this girl. These feelings seemed to overcome my reluctance to ask her for the ultimate pleasure again, but what held me back, was knowing that Alexis had been a virgin and I was the only man she had been with, how was I to suggest to her to comply with my request for more of what we had just shared? I just had to gather the courage and ask her gently. I looked down at her angelic face, with her eyes closed, as she breathed shallowly as if asleep. "Alexis, are you awake?" I asked. Her eyelids fluttered open, and she smiled up at me, "I just closed my eyes for a moment, remembering what had just happened between us and how much I love you, Martin." She could see I was struggling with something and again she asked me, "What is wrong? Is it something I did?" "No Pet, the culmination of our love in the shower was everything I could ever experience, and I want to repeat that beautiful experience." At this comment, she raised herself up onto her elbow and, with a quizzical frown on her face she replied, "Darling, you don't need my permission to make love to me again." She placed her fingers under my chin, and as we gazed into each other's eyes, I explained, in detail, what she meant to me. The silence was broken by a quiet whisper from her, "Martin, I know that what we experienced was something precious and beautiful, and I want to repeat that performance over and over again. Remember, I promised you something very special for your birthday and I don't want to go back on my promise to you."

Words could never explain how she made me feel and I knew, there and then, I had met my soul mate. As we sat ensconced holding each other in a tight embrace, I began to explain to her what it meant for a man to receive the ultimate prize of making love to one whom you cherish most in this world. Again, placing her hands on each side of my face, her soft eyes answered, before her lips said, "Yes. Only if you will be my teacher, I will be your willing student." At that, she agreed to follow my instructions on the art of making true love. The time passed slowly, and to my utter joy, she seemed to gain confidence by following my lead, and it was evident that she was enjoying these ministrations.

That afternoon was emblazoned in my brain, as the most spectacular moments of my young life. Upon leaving the house, we could smell the aroma of the wet seaweed, as it mixed with the salt air wafting in from the ebbing tide. The spectacular late golden sunset cast against the overcast sky amplified the colours' tenfold, which somehow added to the beauty of the night. The only sounds to be heard were the waves lapping over the sand. This was our cue to take off our shoes and begin walking along the cool wet sand at the end of the surf's reach. She put her arm around my waist and held me tight as we walked. I returned in kind, as Alexis rested her head on my shoulder, while we slowly strolled along the beach. It was almost dark when we reached the point at the mouth of the harbour. Crabs chased by the surf, skittered up the beach and, as we were about to turn back, she stopped me. Looking deeply into my eyes, she was silent. I opened my mouth to speak, but she quickly covered it with her hand. Taking the brooch, which she kept in her pocket, she lovingly gazed at my precious gift, before gently cupping my face in her hands and placing her lips on mine. It was as though all fetters of her repressed upbringing were unlocked; making her want to do all the forbidden things she would normally struggle against. She had such a passion burning within her, and now she was no longer reluctant to set it free.

I felt a drop of something wet on my cheek; it was not a tear this time, as it was cold. Then another drop fell and then a heavy shower of rain began. Thunder rolled in the distance, and a jagged streak of lightning split the darkness far out over the water. Alexis looked up at the sky and laughed. She loved the rain and, to her, a thunderstorm was heaven. She kissed me again, as a wry smile curled her lips. Taking my hands in hers, she danced around me in a circle, giggling, her wet dress clinging to her as the rain poured down harder. Dizzy, we both fell on the wet sand, kissing and laughing. Straddling me, she looked down into my eyes, her face drawn with desperate longing. She quickly began unbuttoning my shirt, I started to protest, but she again covered my mouth with her hand. "No more words tonight. You have already said all I needed to know." She leaned down, and once more began kissing me on the lips. As she began to sit up, I pulled her back down kissing her deeply. She pulled away slightly, and then smiled...I knew there would be no argument. Lightning flashed again, closer, the wind driving the chilly rain hard against our skin. Glancing up, I noticed the beach had emptied because of the storm and we found ourselves suddenly alone. Once more, lightning seemed to light up the sky, prompting Alexis to pull her dress over her head, shaking out her short dark hair, as she dropped the wet garment on the sand. Cold rain slowly trickled down her bare breasts, dripping off the ends of her aroused nipples. I couldn't resist taking a drink. Sitting up, I cupped her breasts in my hands and teased both nipples with my tongue. My hands, covered in wet sand, dragged down her smooth skin, leaving a gritty trail which the rain slowly washed away. She then slid back, grinding her crotch on my still covered erection, sending chills up my spine. I fell back, as she moved further down my legs, and began to unbuckle on my belt. Deftly opening my jeans, she reached inside as another bolt of lightning lit the sky. As the thunder rumbled across the sky, I felt a tingling throughout my body, whether from her touch, or the ferocity of the storm, I did not know, nor did I care. She began moving her hands down towards my ankles, and I felt her slowly tugging and pulling my jeans off. I raised my feet back to help her remove them, before tossing the sodden clothing carelessly to the side. Even the cold drops of rain pouring down on us could not deter our passion. In fact, it seemed to drive us on. She bent forward at the hips, again taking my shaft in her hands; I shivered and lowered my head back onto the sand, as the heat of her mouth encompassed me once more. Her tongue flicking back and forth on the underside of my glans, causing me to tense at the sensations flowing through my body. She pulled away momentarily, her wet tresses dragging across my skin, allowing me to relax slightly, before engulfing me again. I could feel her throat constricting around the head of my swelling member, as she fervently sucked on me.

Another flash of lightning split the air, intensifying the tingling flowing throughout my entire body. Crawling back up to my lips, I could feel her hardened nipples being dragged across my stomach. As she sucked at my lower lip, I rolled her onto her back, before kneeling between her open thighs and rubbing my hand over her belly, down to her welcoming love channel. Her body jerked as my thumb brushed over her swollen clit, and as the pouring rain splashed onto her skin, her throaty cry coerced my yearning. Her hips rocked upwards, as though imploring me to fill her – I obliged and, as she lifted her hips to me, I rubbed the head of my throbbing member against her welcoming hot slit teasingly, as she begged me to enter her. Another crackling bolt of electricity, lighting up the sky, only enhanced our bodies, as they crashed together, causing her to grip me harder pulling me towards her. Now, the adrenalin took over. Our hips quickly found a common rhythm, gaining power and speed to the sound of the ferocious song of wind and thunder. I bent down, kissing her breasts, as her hips gyrated against me. Her hands dug into the sand, screaming her pleasure above the din of the storm. Her legs clenched around my body, as another bolt of lightning drove us on. Falling heavily on her, my hips impacted hers again, as her arms wrapped around my neck, rubbing sand across my shoulders, as our bodies continued to increase the animalistic tempo of our love making.

I kissed her hotly on the nape of her neck, feeling the contact of cold rain on my back and her warm flesh under me. She gasped, her body twitching, as she tightened her legs around me, pulling me further into her. Wind driven waves crashed against the beach and I could feel my legs tense at the rush of my orgasm, her own tell-tale shudders gave me the announcement of her own. She cried out once more, as our bodies reached their crescendo with our nerves jangling from the mix of rapture and nature. Lying tangled and senseless, with our hearts pounding and breathing rapidly, the storm quickly blew over and it was some time before either of us had the strength to move. Soon the clouds parted and, as the moon lit the beach, we gathered ourselves together and hurried along towards the caravan. On the Sunday afternoon, our premature honeymoon came to an end.

As we travelled back home, we both realised this was the start of a promising future together. Now the dark clouds slowly descended upon me, as I remembered I would be leaving Alexis on Monday to begin my unenviable journey to the job in Hull, England for a period of four to six weeks. After we returned to the city, from our ideal weekend, we decided we would go our separate ways home, as Alexis had told her Mother she had been with her girlfriends. I assured her that, upon arrival at my destination down south, I would write to her giving her the address of where to contact me.   As we held each other tightly, savouring our last moments together before breaking the spell, I could hear Alexis begin to stifle a sob. Holding her at arms' length and brushing the tears from her cheek with my thumb, I gently admonished her by saying, "We don't do tears here."

I watched her boarding her bus, then, as she sat at the seat nearest the window, she looked so sad and helpless, as she pressed her hand against the window, before blowing me a kiss as she waved goodbye. I stood there as the bus disappeared, I then pulled my jacket tightly around me, feeling despondent, as a foreboding chill seemed to run through my veins when I recalled what was the greatest 48 hours that I had ever known. At that moment, I physically ached for her body, to once more inhale the scent of her skin, as she pressed her body close to mine and hear her soft moans of ecstasy as she reached the ultimate crescendo of love. It was a heavy heart that accompanied me to bed that night, as I was missing Alexis already.

28

Early Monday morning found me sitting in the waiting room of the station, warming my hands on a polystyrene cup of hot tea, having made arrangements to meet my five workmates there. Once we had all gathered and found an empty carriage on the train, it was a case of reading the morning papers, or discussing what had happened over the weekend. I was too engrossed of what had occurred with Alexis, to add anything to the conversation. Once we reached our destination at Hull, we quickly found a small bed and breakfast hotel at the corner of Charles Street, near the Freetown way. The Bed and Breakfast was run by an elderly Welsh lady, a Mrs. Williams, whom we found to be most jovial and welcoming. The rent of our room was very reasonable and, adding to that, she was a wonderful cook. She had two women who assisted her with cleaning and other chores, and when one of them took me to the room that I would be sharing with one of my workmates, the first thing I did was to unpack and get letters off to Alexis and my mother telling them I had arrived safely and giving them my forwarding address.

For the next few days, I would hurry home from the job site where we were installing the new heating system, to see if any mail had been delivered for me, and I found it quite strange that nothing had come. Everyone seemed to be getting letters from home, except for me, but this didn't deter me from continuing to write to Alexis. I was sure she had been sending her letters, as promised, and perhaps there had been some sort of hold up with the post.

It was now three weeks since I had seen Alexis off at the bus station and still hadn't heard from her and I had a gut-wrenching feeling that something was wrong, as I had now written over a dozen letters, without a reply. Over the coming days, the men seemed to notice something was bothering me and one of them tried to cheer me up by saying "No news is good news, at least you've not had a Dear John, so that's something". On the Friday night, as I arrived home from work, Mrs. Williams handed me a letter, smiling as she said, "I think this is what you've been waiting for son." Even she had an idea of what was causing me to be downcast when she noticed I hadn't been receiving any mail. I was all fingers and thumbs, as I hurriedly opened the envelope, but my excitement died the moment I opened the envelope, it was from my mother asking how things were and to thank me for the few pounds I had been sending her from my wages.

That night in bed, sleep wouldn't come as I couldn't get to sleep for the thoughts that were running through my mind. I began to question myself; did I push Alexis too far with my advances towards her? Did I coerce her into doing the things that she had found unpleasant, but went along with it, just to please me, and was now ashamed of what she had done and couldn't bring herself to face me ever again? I resigned myself to the fact that I had thrown away the most precious thing that I had ever had and now I was left with only memories of what might have been. This seemed to make me homesick and I couldn't wait to get back to my friends fast enough, I even thought that going back to the camera club would help take my mind off this sad episode that continued to haunt me.

29

At last, the job had been completed and, when I arrived back home, the first thing on my mind was to see my mother and I was taken aback to find her in bed. She said she was just a bit under the weather, but I didn't realise how ill she really was. While I sat with her, enjoying a proper cup of steaming hot tea, I asked her to tell me all that had happened since I had been away. She gave me all the usual local gossip of who was in hospital, or who had died and who had been asking how I was getting on. If truth be told, I couldn't get on for falling off, as I tried to rid myself of this depressing feeling of not being able to get in touch with Alexis.

After emptying my suitcase and placing some clothes, that I needed washed, in the laundry bag, I decided to go out for a walk and maybe meet up with some of my pals. I had just got to the end of the street and who should come around the corner but my sister Anne with two of her friends and, on seeing me; her first words were "Hi stranger, when did you get back?" She then introduced me to her friends, one of whom worked with Anne, and now had a job in the Tax office and, as luck would have it; she lived across the street from Alexis's family. We stood and talked for a while, before she told me they were in a bit of a hurry as they were going to the cinema and she would catch up with me later. That night, I waited for Anne to come back from the cinema, to ask her to find out from her friend if she had by any chance seen or heard anything about Alexis. When Anne returned home, we sat and chatted for a while, before I asked her to find out what she could about Alexis from her friend, as I wanted to find out if there was any chance of getting in touch with her again, even if it was only to apologise for causing her any pain.

That was on the Friday night and on Sunday, after dinner, Anne waited until my mother had fallen asleep before quietly saying, "I'll have to talk to you later." That night, I noticed that Anne had become very quiet and fidgety, as though she had something on her mind and was stuck for words. I found this unusual, as she had always something to talk about. Then I noticed that she was on the verge of tears, suddenly she looked at me and said "Look Martin, there's no easy way to tell you this, so prepare yourself for a shock. The girl who works with me in the office told me that Alexis had left home and gone to America." My mind went blank and I felt drained of all feeling. Only after I had gained my composure, did I realise what really hurt was finding out from someone else. This was out of character for Alexis, why didn't she let me know personally? I had a gut feeling that something was sadly wrong, but now, as she was in another part of the world, I had to accept I would never find out her reason for leaving. I would be lying if I said there was not hurt, only an emptiness that I had never felt before, but I can still remember to this day. Now I had to rely on "Nurse Time" to bring me some solace, as there was no balm for this pain. I once read that to find the future, one must put aside the past and take an optimistic stance, and this is what I now intended to do.

That same night, I plucked up the courage and took my first leap of faith by going, cap in hand, to confide in my mother and tell her that I had given the Topaz butterfly to Alexis, in place of an engagement ring and now, as she had left home and gone to America, it appears that I shall never see her, nor the Butterfly, again. What kept gnawing at my brain was the thought of the trust my mother had shown me, and now I had to explain how foolish I had been and ask her forgiveness. As I sat at the edge of my mother's bed, she looked so tired and worn out, and now, here I was, having to explain to her what had transpired, but instead of rebuking me, she only smiled as she said, "Don't be too hard on yourself, son. The Topaz Butterfly was yours from the start and it will find its own way home, it always has." Those words stayed with me throughout all the qualms and traumas that I encountered, as I made my way in life.

I began by going back to college again to take advanced lessons on photography in the hope that, someday, I would become a professional photographer and earn a living by doing the type of work that has always appealed to me.

30

Alexis's life story

After spending such a glorious weekend with my one true love, Martin, I made my way home to my own family. This was something I was not looking forward to, as my mother always seemed to be constantly questioning me where I had been and what I had been up to. It was as if she was trying to live her life through me, but, at the same time, she kept a tight rein on me. My Mother had had a hard life, but, if the truth be known, most mothers during that era seemed to have a life of drudgery, having babies, raising them, while the men earned the wages and handed in what they deemed appropriate for the wife to raise the family and keep a home going.

I hated lying to my mother by telling her that I had spent the weekend at my friend's family cottage down by the seaside, but I would never have been allowed to go away with Martin. First of all, any boyfriend of mine would be taboo to her. I didn't have any boyfriend to speak of, all of my friends were either going out with their friends, or going to the dance nights at the local social clubs, in the housing estate where we lived, also I was a babysitter for my younger siblings, after I came home from work.

When I arrived home from my weekend at Kathleen's vacation home, everyone was just finishing their evening meal and, of course, when I came through the door, the younger ones were clamouring over me to find out if I had brought them a treat. I did stop by the local newsagents and bought some of their favourite sweeties, which was always special to them. I carefully put my clothes away and changed into my pyjamas, washed my face and prepared for the grilling I knew I would be receiving from my mother (since my father was working down in England, so she had sole responsibility for all of us). Just as I had expected, it didn't take long for my mother to start questioning me about my weekend and what had taken place. She seemed to take a delight in browbeating me, but I knew she was worried because of the responsibility which was placed on her shoulders keeping us on the "straight and narrow" while my father was absent. All I could think of was getting to bed and going over what had transpired between Martin and me over the past two days. It took some time before falling asleep that night, as my head was buzzing with all that had taken place between me and Martin, the special man who had awakened a hunger in me that I had never known before. Now I could start planning my future with him.

The days slowly crept by and each night, when I returned home from work, my expectations were soaring with the thought of receiving a letter from Martin, as he had promised to write to me. But my hopes were dashed each night when my mother would tell me there was no mail at all. This was hard to comprehend, as I knew Martin had promised me he would write and I knew, instinctively, he would not go back on his word. "Martin, my beloved Martin, where are you?" The thoughts of my precious Martin swirled around and around in my brain. It had been almost two months since we parted – as he was going down south for four to six weeks, working on installing heating equipment in a new school, which was being built in Hull. We both promised to keep in touch, but I hadn't heard a peep from him.

I asked my mother; when I returned from work each day, if any mail had come for me, and I would always receive a curt response, with a sneer, saying "Nothing today. As I have told you Alexis, many times, don't hang your dreams on him. He is probably having a grand old time and not even giving you a thought." She seemed to spit those words from her mouth. I brushed past her, as the tears were smarting behind my eyes and I didn't want her to see my resolve weaken. I made for the bedroom and lay on my bed. By now, the tears were rolling down my cheeks, "Surely not, Martin, please don't make her words be real," I sobbed into my pillow. Of course, no one would be good enough for me…. because to my mother I was an extra pay packet coming into the house. As each day passed, and not hearing from him, I became afraid. I had missed my period and now a new worry was placed on my shoulders. Could I be pregnant? Panic set in, what was I to do? Rubbish the thought, I said to myself. Martin and I had made love only twice that beautiful weekend, the weekend before he left for his new assignment. Up until then, I was a virgin and to think that from those two instances, surely I was not pregnant!

As I lay there, I started making plans. First of all, if I was pregnant, I had to start making those plans now. It had always been a dream of mine to leave Glasgow, because in my mind, there was nothing there for me. Again, if I was pregnant, that would put a wrench in my plans. So began my odyssey into the unknown. I was worked for a large corporation, Caterpillar Tractor, as an Executive Secretary to the President of this organization. Mr. Salter, who was an American, had moved to Glasgow to set up this plant, which was to be located in a small town outside of Glasgow. I had been hired, from the very beginning of this new venture in Glasgow, to work for him and, although he was my boss, he was also a friend. I had shared with him my goal in life to go to America and he seemed pleased that I had the gumption to venture out on this journey by myself. This is when I began to formulate my plans.

I had a meeting with Mr. Salter and he said he would help me. First of all, he would arrange for me to stay with one of his family members in Chicago, who would sponsor me, and then help me find a job. Of course, I didn't divulge the fact that I might be pregnant. I would cross that bridge when I came to it. I had been saving for some time and had enough money to pay for my one-way fare to Chicago, Illinois, with some money left to tide me over until I secured a job there. I had sworn him to secrecy, as I didn't want anyone to know where and when I was leaving.

31

My family life carried on as normal, until the day the package, containing my passport and other formal documentation, arrived at the office where I worked. I had requested this be done, in order that my mother would not be suspicious of my plans. I checked out that all my papers were in order, my flight ticket was accurate; I had withdrawn all of what little money I had left from the bank and closed my account.

It was now Sunday evening and my family had all gone to visit my grandparents and I was left alone. This was when I had filled a small suitcase with what meagre clothing I had and took the bus to a friend's home. I had told her I was going on a short trip down to England and I didn't want to take my suitcase to work. I returned home and went straight to bed. I couldn't sleep, my mind was churning. Why had Martin failed to contact me? Was it true, did he think I was a "one-night stand" and took advantage of me. Surely not, I loved this wonderful, kind, handsome young man all my life and that fabulous night we made love, was truly the culmination of our love. In my heart, I believed this and that something had to have happened to Martin and he was unable to reach me. I chided myself for ruminating useless thoughts.... I knew that I had to leave Glasgow in the event I was pregnant. I couldn't place this added burden upon my family, as we had enough mouths to feed, without another being added to the mix.

My flight was leaving on Monday night. Before leaving in the morning, I had written a short note to my mother, telling her I would be leaving for a short vacation and I would write her a letter when I arrived at my destination. Then, I stopped by my friend's home Monday morning, retrieved my suitcase and headed for the airport. Mr. Salter had given me the names of his family members, who seemed very happy to help me and they would meet me at O'Hare Airport. I had a whole day to kill, until the flight left for the United States. To say I was nervous was an understatement. But, there was a sense of excitement too. My dream was coming to fruition; I had excellent skills at my fingertips, good references from Mr. Salter (he had been an excellent mentor for me, filling me in on how life would be like in his country, much different that I had experienced in Glasgow). So, I decided to make the most of this, be confident and meet every challenge that life would throw my way.

32

I had never flown in my life and this was truly a nightmare flight. I was so sick and the stewardess had brought me a total of six airsick bags. They must have thought "What a wimp, she is." I wondered if this was the result of air motion sickness, or the fact that I may have been pregnant. Nevertheless, I persevered and we landed in New York City, which was a stopover, before carrying on to Chicago. I went into a little café in LaGuardia Airport and asked the waitress for a cup of tea. It was stifling hot when we landed and she brought me this glass of amber coloured water. I said to her, "Miss, this tea is cold." She looked at me oddly and said, "Of course, Miss, it is iced tea." I had never tasted, never mind heard of iced tea. Although I must say, it was delicious, and the lemon slice flavoured it nicely. After a two-hour layover, we boarded another plane and headed for my destination, Chicago. Mr. Salter's brother, James and his wife Sally met me and immediately their affection for me was palpable. Then and there I knew I had made the right move. Their car was huge and luxurious with tinted green windows…. I felt I was in the movies.

As we drove away from O'Hare Airport, I drank in all the hustle and bustle of the largest airport in the United States. The drive down the Dan Ryan Expressway (eight lanes of traffic) was mind-boggling. It seemed that there were hundreds of cars, flowing smoothly in each lane, and the skyscraper buildings were on each side of this magnificent highway. My mind was trying to take all of this in and it left me breathless. Eventually, we left the busy highway and the skyscraper buildings and moved into lush greenery and beautiful, spacious homes in the suburbs. James and Sally helped me into their lovely home and I met their two young daughters. It truly was an exciting time for me and they made me so welcome, it was as if I was a long, lost family member. Wow, who would have believed that only 24 hours before I was a bag of nerves, sitting in Prestwick Airport where the rain was lashing against the windows and the wind was howling like a banshee. Now, the sun was shining, and I was in the midst of a family who welcomed me to their country with open arms. There surely was a God in Heaven who was looking out for me.

We ate a light supper, as I was still recuperating from the bout of airsickness on the flight. Then James informed me that he had set up an interview with a friend of his, Don Sullivan, who was the Personnel Manager of a large trucking outfit, Gateway Transportation. I smiled at him with love in my heart, would there be no end to the kindness shown to me? After we retired for the night, I lay on my new bed and I said a sincere prayer of thanks to God for all His blessings bestowed upon me. Now, I had to make sure, first and foremost, that I needed to secure a job, then find out if I was pregnant or not, and start my new and wonderful life in this magnificent city of Chicago. Before I succumbed to sleep, my thoughts dwelled on my beloved Martin....... where was he? Did he really mean all that he said to me about being so in love with me? I was heartbroken and fraught with fear and insecurity. Was I up for this challenge, which was unfolding in front of my eyes? I did make a promise to myself that I would do everything in my power to find Martin again.... I didn't have a plan, but I was full of bravado making this promise to myself.

The interview with Mr. Sullivan was a success and I was hired to start the next day, at a salary four times what I made as a secretary in Glasgow. Life was running smoothly for me at last. My memory of Martin would always be with me. I still loved this man fervently and would do so until I took my last breath. I knew if I wanted to move forward, I would have to take one step at a time.   Sally Salter had me register with her doctor (I had to let her know what my concern was, and she assured me she would keep my secret in confidence, until I told her otherwise). After a few days, the doctor confirmed I was three months pregnant. What to do now? First of all, I had a meeting with Mr. Sullivan, my boss, to inform him what I had been told. He was so kind too (my entire experience with Americans, is that they are the most loving, kind and caring people in this world). Knowing that I did not have medical insurance (one must be employed three months with a company before benefits become eligible). So, he arranged for me to have a meeting with a surgeon friend of his who worked at the University of Illinois Teaching Hospital. They accepted me as a patient, with one caveat, I would be sort of a "guinea pig," meaning that I would be assigned a doctor throughout my pregnancy, with about a dozen interns viewing every move he made when I had a visit, hence a "teaching hospital."

Now that all my plans were falling into place: I had a great job, good friends and my healthcare was taken care of, what more could I ask for? But there was more, much more. My heart was heavy having lost touch with my beloved Martin. I was so sure that something must have happened. Having known him all of my life, this behaviour of not hearing from him, was baffling, because I knew in my heart his love for me was as strong as mine was for him. But, since I had left Scotland without anyone knowing what my plans were to emigrate and now living in Illinois, how was he ever going to find me, if he wanted to find me? I put this concern to the back of my mind temporarily, and knew, once I was settled, I would address it at that time. I had to take baby steps until I could decide what was the best way to move forward.

33

Sally helped me find a small apartment, which was close to public transportation making access to my job more amenable. I then wrote to my mother telling her where I was, omitting the knowledge of my pregnancy, as this was my life now and I had promised myself that I would not divulge this, until the time was right. Of course, she was enraged at the "sleekit way" I had formulated my plan. She also said not to write to her anymore, she was finished with me. Now, I was really on my own, familywise that is. I settled in very well at my new job, as I learned that Americans always loved the fact that they had a Scottish Executive Secretary working for them. If the truth be known, I worked very hard to prove myself and it convinced my boss, Don Sullivan and the assistant Personnel Manager, Mr. Pucci, when they told me that the office ran like clockwork since I arrived and, for once, all the filing was up-to-date! When I first filled out my employment application, the questions were very personal i.e. how much did I weigh (in Scotland, our measures were in pounds and stones) so I put that down, and Mr. Pucci, for months afterwards, would tease me and ask how many stones did I weigh now? I had never experienced such an informal atmosphere in a corporate environment. This helped me settle down much quicker than I thought I would.

My pregnancy was effortless, there was no morning sickness, I looked after my weight and diet and walked whenever I could, and things ran quite smoothly, I fretted so much about Martin, as I kept wracking my brain on what could have gone wrong. But, the unknown fear of thinking I was pregnant, overtook everything as in those days, particularly in Scotland, an unmarried girl was taboo and, many times, they were sent away from their home town to await the birth of their baby, which normally would be put up for adoption. If I was pregnant, I knew I would NEVER give up my child…. this child was created by Martin and me and he would be my most precious child. So strong was my conviction on this dilemma, it made me forge ahead with my plans to move away from Glasgow, and that culminated in my decision to go to the United States.

When the time arrived for the birth of my child, it was my last week working with Mr. Sullivan, and the staff had a farewell party for me. They had bought me a beautiful pram, a highchair, a layette and an envelope stuffed with dollar bills. What did I say about the kindness of Americans? In my short time living in Chicago, I had made so many beautiful friendships, that the heartbreak of not knowing the whereabouts of Martin eased somewhat in my heart.

Returning home from that surprise party with all the lovely gifts, I sat down in my little apartment, holding my extended stomach, whispering to my little child that, he or she, would be given a good life with me. This promise would never be broken! It was just the two of us now. A few days later, I had my final visit with my doctor, who informed me that the baby was easing down into the birth canal. The following morning, I started having twinges of pain, which was unusual for me. I telephoned the nurse, who asked me, "How much time between the contractions?" I replied, "They are every minute." She then instructed me to come directly to the hospital – I was in labour!! Since I didn't have a car, I gathered my little suitcase and walked up the street and took the bus to the hospital. Once I was checked in, they prepared me for delivery and put me into a ward filled with all black girls, who were in various stages of labour. The air was blue with their cursing, as each pain penetrated their bodies. Actually, in retrospect, it was funny, because here I was, the only white girl, not uttering a sound. I had learned to grasp the steel railing of the bed and counted to 30, as each pain coursed through my body. I swear I left my fingerprints on these bars. What was the sense of screaming, the nurses had enough to do, without listening to the curses of these young ladies? I laboured for about ten hours and then my son, Martin Jr., was born, coming into the world at 12 pounds, 25 inches long. He came into this world screaming and kicking and the doctor told me he would make a great soccer player one of these days. In those days, a patient only stayed three days and then was discharged.

34

Since I was on my own, the only people who came to pick me up were James and Sally Salter. We were still friends and, in a kind of way, they were surrogate parents to me. We arrived back at my apartment and, true to form, Sally had prepared for our homecoming by setting up a crib, food in the refrigerator and a lovely hot meal prepared for us. The generosity of these true friends was a blessing to me. After settling us in, they departed and once again, I was alone with my son and my memories of Martin, my soulmate, who, for whatever reason, had stopped communicating with me. Marty (as I called my son now) was such a good baby, great nature (somewhat like his father) and he was so much like Martin with his jet-black hair and big brown eyes. I had made another friend, Mrs. Mack, who lived next door to my apartment. She had a Downs Syndrome child, Rainey, who adored Marty and, whenever we went out for a walk in his pram, Rainey would gush over him, Marty reciprocated by grabbing her finger and holding on. This pleased Mrs. Mack and she told me that if I ever wanted to return to work, she would willingly look after Marty. This was a godsend for me, as my funds were running low (there was no unemployment compensation at that time).

I then applied for a position at Campbell Soup, as Executive Secretary in Personnel. This, too, was a successful interview and I started working when my son was a little over a year old. The transition of leaving him in the capable of hands of Mrs. Mack was heart-wrenching for both of us, but I had to start earning money again. It was a great job and I was quickly promoted, and my salary grew to the extent I was now in the position to purchase a second-hand car. The social life in this company was alive and well, however, being a single parent this was not conducive to my life-style, so I usually deferred from any invitations. Mrs. Mack, again another kindly mother-like figure, told me she was worried about me and that I should start going out with friends, she wouldn't mind looking after Marty for the odd night.

One afternoon, the group from the office were stopping off for pizza after work and I was invited. I called Mrs. Mack and arranged for her to keep my son for an extra couple of hours.   It was at this event that I met this fellow, Josh. He was older, but had a quiet demeanour about him. We struck up a conversation and, before we knew it, the time had come to say goodnight. He wanted to see me again and we set a date. He knew about my son, but didn't inquire any further into my background, not that I was going to divulge this to anyone! Soon, this relationship became routine, but I didn't love him, because I had given my heart to someone else, and that would never change. I think Josh realized this. Still, he persevered and persuaded me to marry him so that he could give security to both Marty and me. We set the date and were married quietly, with just a few friends attending the ceremony. It didn't take long for me to realize my mistake. Josh had a split personality...nice and quiet on the outside, then when he had a drink, his ugly side was exposed. Of course, there were lots of apologies in the morning. The derogatory insults were very demeaning and they took their toll on me. Of course, no one was aware of this. This was my ugly secret and was concealed to the outside world. My biggest worry was my son, and how it could affect him. Although still a child, it is a known fact that children are very perceptive and relationships with them are supposed to be nurturing and loving. One blessing was that Josh travelled a lot with his job and thus would only be home one week out of four. I tried everything to make life easier for us, but to no avail. He found fault with everything and it seemed that I was always to blame for whatever upset him. When Josh was out of town, I always made a point of making time to do special things with Marty. On the weekends (weather permitting), we would take day trips to the Indiana Dunes, where we would spend the entire day on the beach, splashing in the water and just having a happy time. My son was the most important person to me now. Protecting him, at all costs, was my priority.

As the days, weeks and months passed, my memories of Martin were just as poignant as ever, however, I was still at a loss at how he vanished from my life….I was confident in my heart that his love for me was as strong as mine was for him, but (and there always seems to be a BUT) for the life of me, I couldn't fathom his decision not to get in touch with me.

As time passed, I could feel my thoughts and images of him were put to the back of my mind. I struggled to keep my memories of him fresh in my mind until, one day, while cleaning out some of my closets; I came across my small jewellery box. I didn't wear much jewellery these days (couldn't afford much) and resorted to wearing only a simple pair of gold earrings. I rummaged through what was there and there it was……the most beautiful brooch which Martin had gifted to me as a token of his love for me. It lay there, glittering and twinkling from the overhead light – The Topaz Butterfly. It was then, that the tears flowed once again for my handsome Martin, the man who had such a grip on my heart. I held the precious butterfly to my heart, closing my eyes, I heard Martin voice say to me, "My darling Alexis, I am giving this heirloom to you as a token of my love. You are, and always will be, the only woman whom I will love until I draw my last breath. When we have children, our first born son will, hopefully, present this brooch to his bride and they will carry on the tradition." I crumpled to the floor, clasping the brooch; it was as if the wind had been knocked out of me. My mind was racing once more, what had happened to Martin? What if he had returned to my home in Glasgow and my estranged mother, with her wilful ways, would turn him away and then he would have no idea where I had gone. What was I to do?

I quickly dried my tears, pulled myself together, and carefully wrapped the precious jewellery back in its cocoon of cotton, then gently placed it back on the bottom of the black velvet box. I would try to figure out this dilemma, one way or another. Meanwhile, our life must go on. My routine was to pick up Marty after school, then come home to prepare supper for us. My husband was due home that night from his travelling and it was important to keep the peace in the house. Lately, it was a guessing game what kind of mood he would be in. To be honest, I myself had two personalities: one was quiet, deferential and serene in our home, the other, while at work, was one of supreme confidence, vivacious and someone who "had the world by the tail." I was on a fast-track at work for promotions.

My superiors knew that I was hungry for knowledge and they fed that hunger, while they depended on me for many things. Work was where I flourished! My co-workers knew of my love and devotion to my child, but I never discussed my marriage at all. To them, everything about me was on an even keel. Little did they know my job was what kept me sane, and an all-consuming love for my little Marty, who meant the world to me! I was like a bear protecting her cub.

Marty was a precocious, solitary boy and I felt he sensed the underlying emotions when his step-father entered our home. It was an unwritten code that we were to be on our best behaviour, at all costs, if he suspected Josh had been drinking. In retrospect, I felt shame that my son had to endure this kind of behaviour. But, as the saying goes, hindsight is 20/20. Josh came home this one night, sullen and moody. As usual, he was greeted with hugs and smiles, but this did not assuage him in the least. The meal was eaten in silence, with the odd comment from me asking how his week had gone. All of a sudden, Josh's two fists came crashing down on the table, he shouted, "What the hell do you care how my week went? You and your precious son couldn't give a damn how my week went." I started shaking, pushing my chair back, and mustering up what little courage I had, I responded, "Do you mean to tell me that you don't realize the tension you create by your behaviour when you walk through this door? Both of us are on tenterhooks while you reside under this roof, all because of your boorish behaviour when you drink. To be honest, I am sick of it and, unless you curb this bad habit of yours, you should stay away from us." I sat down with a thump, trying to control the tears that were forming behind my eyes. Where did this come from? Me, who had never confronted this man before, who now sat before me with his mouth wide-open. He was at a loss for words. The silence in the room was palpable, what would happen now? The meal was finished in silence. Marty said, "Mom, I will help you clear the table and put the dishes in the sink." Josh, scraped his chair back from the table, and stalked into the living-room. My son put his little arms around my waist and said, "Don't worry Mom, it had to be said. I think things may change now." Like I said, my son seemed to be prophetic because, that evening Josh apologized for his outburst and went to bed.

The next morning, Josh went back on the road once again and peace reigned in our home once more. I may have silenced him for now, but I was still a little sceptical. Life was peaceful for a while, but the old adage "leopards don't change their spots," rose up to bite me, and Josh resorted back to his old ways. He needed professional help, but that was his decision to make.

Before Marty was born, while going for my regular visits to the doctor at the University of Illinois Hospital, I befriended a young woman, Mary Ann, who would become one of my life-long friends. She was so sweet and, being aware of my situation at home, she helped me in many ways of finding my way around this beautiful, big city of Chicago. It was in times of my distress, with my marriage in particular, that Mary Ann was a shoulder to lean on. She never judged anyone; she just listened, while I struggled for reasons why this was happening to me. She would prove to be a constant in my life.

My married life became, at times, a nightmare, but the vows I had taken "in sickness and in health" became more and more an obstacle. I knew that divorce was out of the question, and Josh wouldn't be going anywhere. I firmly believed he knew I would never leave him, thus giving him the upper hand. He knew that, being the forgiving person I was, I could never live with the consequences of what would happen to him if I did leave him. He took advantage of this and continued on with his drinking and very boorish behaviour. As Marty grew older and taller, he was an excellent student and pursued many sports, namely swimming, karate and baseball. One sport that didn't appeal to him was soccer and, wouldn't you know it, this was one sport that Josh wanted him to learn. This became a sore point for both of them. I firmly believed Marty knew that his step-father wanted him to pursue this sport and, because this was the only subtle way of defying him, he decided in his young mind, "I will not play soccer just to make him happy." Little did my son know, Josh would use this as a weapon against Marty. He would turn his anger towards my son, knowing full well that this was a strike against me. Josh proved to be a very manipulative man. He hoped he could divide and conquer – I mean, what man would resort to this kind of behaviour, when raising such a fine young man as his step-son? At my request, I asked Marty to give it a try just to appease his step-father. He acquiesced and went for a trial. He proved to be an excellent player and, to his surprise, he enjoyed this sport too. However, Josh, in his immature way, failed to support him and never attended any of his games. This was the kind of behaviour I had to endure – it was to become "peace at any price." But, my son, in his infinite wisdom, rose above all of this oafish behaviour displayed by Josh and continued to succeed in all that he attempted.

35

On his sixteenth birthday, Marty was awarded his Black Belt in Karate. What an accomplishment for one so young! But, no matter how accomplished he became, the negative comments spewed from Josh's mouth, Marty would never be good enough in his eyes. This time though, Josh went too far. At 6"4" my son towered over his stepfather, but unbeknownst to me, this was of concern to Josh. Now, he felt he had to curb his tongue when in the company of this young man. One night, Marty was out with his friends and Josh and I sat watching a certain program on TV. Every so often, he would rise out of his chair and disappear into the bar/library on the pretence he was looking up certain things. I was engrossed in this film and didn't notice the change in his behaviour. When he emerged from the room at one point, he pointed his finger at me and ordered me to get ready for bed and to get upstairs. This was utterly preposterous to me and I told him so. He ran over to me, grabbed me by the hair and started dragging me upstairs. I tried to fight back, when suddenly; the front door opened and in walked Marty. He quickly assessed the situation and, upon removing his jacket, he said to Josh, "This time you have gone too far. Take your hands off my Mom, or I will break your neck.' When Josh released me, I crumpled on the stairs, and he retreated backwards down the stairs, blubbering "It isn't what you think it is. You've got the wrong end of the stick, as usual." Marty gently picked me up saying, "Mom, are you OK?" I nodded my head, held onto his arm and whispered, "Don't hurt him, it is the drink.' Marty retorted, "Mom, don't make any more excuses for him. I am sick and tired of you covering for him. Either he shapes up, or ships out." This was an ultimatum and Josh did not take ultimatums. He brushed past both of us and went to bed. My son and I sat up late into the night trying to resolve this dilemma. I knew there was no way Josh would change, but I held out the hope that, when Marty went to University, I could handle myself dealing with this situation. I conveyed this to Marty and, though he knew I could take care of myself, he agreed that maybe when he was at University, Josh would settle down. He knew that he was a threat to his stepfather.

All this drinking took its toll on Josh's health and slowly, slowly his body started rejecting the drink, but the damage was done, he went into cardiac arrest and died peacefully. Shortly before his death, while in hospital, he took my hand and told me, in a hushed whisper, "I am so sorry for all the unhappiness I caused you throughout our marriage." I squeezed his hand and reassured him not to fret. Inside, I told myself "Too little, too late." I contacted Marty of his stepfather's demise and all he could say was, "Mom, now you can start living once again. "Marty excelled in University and came home to visit when he could, and I filled my time with visiting my friend Mary Ann and my job.

36

But, with so much time on my hands when I arrived home, I started thinking about Martin again. He would be 40 years of age now, where was he, what was he doing, was he married? I needed to try and find him, but how? Where would I start? I felt it only right that he be told about his son. I tried writing to his family, but the letters were returned marked "moved, no forwarding address." I knew about the transition of homes in Glasgow, people were being moved out to new housing schemes in the outlying districts of Glasgow. I felt it would be like looking for a needle in a haystack, but I kept this quest to myself, as I didn't think that Marty would want me to be upset. I had given Marty a very short version of who his real father was, but I still felt shame on what had transpired and how I handled the situation. I wasn't going to blame Martin, because I knew in my heart, something went wrong and I was not about to point fingers at anyone, until I found out the truth.

With my son away at University, I continued working, slowly climbing the corporate ladder, so to speak. My social life was obsolete, except for my co-workers, who occasionally went out to the movies or a meal with me. Marty came home regularly, usually with some of his friends tagging along. Some of them lived in residence at the

University, as they came from faraway countries, and only saw their families on Winter and Summer breaks. I encouraged Marty to bring them home with him for a home-cooked meal and a taste of home life. It was great for me, as I enjoyed being with my son, watching him grow into a fine young man, responsible, kind and dedicated to his studies. His life at the University was hard work and determination, knowing he was working towards his goal, at that time, of being a Veterinarian. His love of animals and wild-life was synonymous with his nature, and with his biological father, Martin who was gentle, yet strong, and memories of Martin came flooding back....the young man who had entered into my life for a brief time, then who completely vanished from it, without a trace.

37

My memories of Martin, though somewhat faded, still burned brightly in a little corner of my heart. He would be 42 years of age now, what had become of him? With all ties cut from the "old Country" there was no way of me finding out anything about him. Had he, like me, got on with his life? Was he happily married with a family now? I would never know, would I? There were times when Mary Ann and I would go out for a meal and we would discuss where life was taking us. For me, there was a void, knowing full well it had to be filled. My son was growing into everything I had hoped he would be. Yet, I knew there would come a time when he would want answers to really know who his real father was, and he was determined to find him. I was reluctant to think about this, as my heart had been closed off from those wonderful memories for years now, and I just wanted to "let sleeping dogs lie."

This was the year that Marty would be graduating from University with a Batchelor of Science degree, and he had been accepted into the University of Illinois Veterinary School of Medicine. Soon, he would realize his dream of being a Veterinarian, but he would have another four years of study to complete his DVM degree.   I had saved a little money each payday, to be put into an educational fund for him and thus he was not to suffer the burden of loans for his education. He had received many scholarships, which helped greatly, and when his education was completed, he would be free of any debt.

38

Martin's Story

For the past few years of attending college, I eventually got my Bachelor of Arts degree in Photography and upon hearing my name, being summoned to the podium, was one of the proudest moments of my life, and that was the moment I realised this could give me the opportunity to follow my hopes of becoming a professional photographer. The only drawback was, should I take the chance of leaving my current job to pursue a career in photography? I was now 25, single and without any responsibilities, but was I willing to leave my present job which guaranteed me a good weekly wage, to go looking for my dream? I pondered this quandary over the next few days and ended up by asking "Scoop" for his advice and his words to me were, "You're the only person who can make that choice Martin, but all I can say is, if you stay here indefinitely, in later years you'll always question yourself, "Could have, would have, should have." I know I often did.

The following week my problem was resolved in the most unexpected way. It was on a Tuesday morning when the complete workforce was told to make their way to the main office and, when we were all gathered there, the rumours went into overdrive. The first thing I thought of was there was going to be a change in the work, or shift system, or there would be no pay rise. A short while later, in came the shop steward with young Mr. Gallagher, the owner's son, following behind. "Gentlemen, I have some very sad news and it's only proper that you should all be first to know what's about to take place. Over the past few months, most of our contracts have been cancelled due to the recent financial climate, so to keep our heads above water, and after much deliberation to find a solution; we have come to the sad conclusion that four workers will be made redundant." That short sentence started a babbling noise that filled the office, with the older engineers making the loudest protests, "Where will ah' get another joab at my age?" or, "We've got a mortgage tae pay." Then a loud shout cut through the cacophony of noise "Lads, lads, settle doon." It was the shop steward, "Let the man finish before goin' aff the deep end." It fell to a quiet mumble, as the owner's son carried on what was about to take place. "I have had talks with your union reps and we came up with what we thought was a solution to this unfortunate incident. The plan is that if four men volunteer to accept redundancy, they can work for another month, giving them a chance to look for an opening with another company, plus the fact they shall be receiving a good redundancy package to tide them over until they find other employment. It also helps me from having the unfortunate task of choosing four men, some of whom I've known over many years. You have until the weekend to think about this, before I have to choose." At that very moment on hearing this, I thought to myself. Here's the answer to my dilemma and it's getting handed to me on a plate, I have a complete month to, hopefully, find a job with some company connected to photography."

As we left the office, I made a beeline for "Scoop" to tell him what I was about to do and when I caught up with him, before I could say a word, he said, "You're going for it, I guessed you would and, if I was your age, I would've done the same, but noo' you have only a month to get yourself sorted oot. Ah know that you'd like a job that would gie' ye' a chance tae make a livin' using yer camera, ah'm no promisin' anything, but ah know a few guys from the camera club that dae just that, so ah'll have a word wi' some o' them and, in the meantime, check oot some o' the camera magazines, as sometimes they advertise for staff.

Three weeks passed and my hopes of getting a job that consisted of being a photographer looked bleak, it seemed that I would be looking for another engineering post, or anything else that happened to pass my way. I would be let go by the firm on the Friday, with a tidy sum of money from my redundancy and, after sharing some of the cash with my mother, I still had enough money to tide me over for a few weeks. I realised I had to get another job fast, but vacancies for heating engineers were few and far between.

It was like a scene from the movies, when the cavalry arrives in the nick of time to win the battle and save the day, only this time 'Scoop' was my cavalry. When he sat at my table, two days before I said my farewell to those who were staying with the firm, "Ah' think we cracked it Martin, I spoke to one o' the boys called Jackie McPhee, who still uses the club's equipment, although he is now out on his own, setting up booths in different shopping centres, making good money by taking baby and family group photo's. Ah had a word wi' him and he's quite keen tae meet ye'. Ah gave ye' a good write-up so it's up tae you now, ah'n ah know ye' won't let me down." Scoop then told me he had made an appointment for me to meet the chap McPhee down in the camera club on Wednesday night at 7 o'clock and bring some of my photos that I had taken, with me. This was the chance I had been hoping for and I really wanted to impress by taking some of my best work with me. There were a mixture of portraits, scenic views and shots of different parts of the city.

I got to the club early and didn't take my eyes off the door, waiting for this stranger to appear and the best way to approach him. I needn't have bothered, for who should turn up but Scoop, along with the chap he wanted me to meet. "This is Jackie, Martin, so I'll leave you two to get oan wi' it "said Scoop "and ah'l see you baith later." "Well Martin, Scoop told me you're wanting to try your hand at the photography business? I must start by telling you, it can be hard going and not as easy as some folks would have you believe. I notice you brought some of your work with you, so can I have a look at them?" After going through them one by one, he said he was quite impressed, although he said there were some little things I should work on and proceeded to point them out to me. This was good advice, as it would help me to hone my skills at using the camera, to get the best results from every shoot. He then offered me a job, on a temporary basis, to see how I would adapt to this type of work, and if I had the temperament to photograph children who often had to be pacified, prior to having their photo taken. Just before we all left, Scoop shook me warmly by the hand and told me not to be a stranger and come back and see the other workers whenever I felt like it. Jackie then asked me to meet him on Saturday at the Mall, where he would be taking portraits, to give me an idea of what was entailed when setting up for a shoot.

On the Saturday, I looked on as Jackie sat a child on an array of brightly coloured cushions and, before going behind the tripod which held the camera, the fun began, as he held cuddly toys in his hand, moving it in all directions to get the child's attention. It usually was a success and, nine times out of ten, it worked, but there was always that one who stubbornly refused to sit, or bawled its head off, making it impossible to get the photo.

After we finished for the day, Jackie asked "Well what do you think? I know it looks quite simple, every mother thinks her baby, especially the girls, are the cutest little things since Shirley Temple and you've got to go along with that and agree with her, because every photo means money, so do think you can handle it?" I didn't hesitate, "Yes, I believe I can, this type of photography won't faze me, in fact, I'm looking forward to the hands-on and practical side of the job. "This seemed to meet his approval and he said, "Good, that's what I like to hear, so I'm going to let you take over on your own tomorrow, as I'm covering for one of the other guys who can't make it. I'll be at the other mall if you run into any problems, so don't worry".

The gods really smiled on me that Sunday, it was a beautiful sunny day with all the children dressed in their summery outfits and dresses. I had just set up the cameras and lights, before placing previous photos of young babies and children on the large picture board, when a young couple with a young baby in a pushchair came over and asked if I would take his child's photo. This was a special moment for me; this could become my first step on the ladder rung to become a paid photographer. Everything worked out perfectly; the baby was an ideal model, happily sitting there with a wonderful smile as if it knew this was my very first shoot. The rest of the day seemed to go by in a blur, at times, there were two to three ladies standing in line to get their little darlings photographed, so that in years to come they could remember how they shone on that wonderful day.

I met Jackie on the Monday night and he was really impressed by what I had achieved, in fact, he asked me if I was interested in going to a couples' home to take a family portrait. I didn't have to be asked twice and jumped at the chance. Again, it was just a matter of making the family feel at ease, the only problem was getting the youngest boy, who was adamant and reluctant to get his photo taken unless he could wear his favourite football strip. I soon got around that by taking two photos, one in his strip and one without. The parents took the photo of the one, minus the football strip.

Over the coming months, I was making good wages, plus commission, working part-time for Jackie, plus I was always on hand to work freelance, taking wedding photos and supplying the albums for the wedding parties. Once more, I enrolled in the local college of commerce and took a three-year study course on advanced photography and journalism. Working through the day with Jackie and studying at night, played havoc with the little social life I had, but I was willing to make this sacrifice until I got my next degree, which I finally did.

39

Now that I had reached the age of 28, I was more determined than ever to be my own boss, so I contacted the local council and was fortunate enough to get a contract to take all the class photos in the district.   I also had many of the official council functions to cover. It was hard work, but the financial rewards more than made up for that. Everything was going just the way I had planned, a good bank balance and a promising future ahead of me, not bad for a 28 year old. Although, when I thought about it, I often wondered was it all worth it, giving up what social life I had, and missing good times with my friends? Now, most of my friends were married and were living the domestic life, but that didn't appeal to me. I wanted to be my own man, happy with my lot, and with no one to answer to and free to do as I pleased.

That came to a sudden end, when my mother was taken into hospital with what I thought was a minor ailment, What I didn't realise was how ill she really was, until on a visit to the hospital my sister and I were told by the doctor who was attending to her that her illness was terminal, how could this be? I never heard her once complain, she must have struggled to put a brave face and keep smiling when we were with her. My mother lasted for two weeks, before succumbing to her illness, but it was a godsend, as she didn't suffer too long. She was a good living soul, always there to help anyone if she could, she never missed attending Church on weekdays and Sundays, so my sister and I thought it only proper that she should be taken from the church to be interred in the Catholic cemetery.

There was a sparse amount of people who turned up, mostly aunts, uncles and the few friends that she had. After the burial, as we were leaving the cemetery, the Priest caught up with me as I was walking away. He tapped me on the shoulder and as I turned around to face him he said "Your mother was a fine woman, never missed Mass and..." "Let me stop you there" I spat out, "You didn't know her, or even attempt to try to get to know my mother. When did you last visit her at home, or even take the time to visit her on her deathbed in the hospital? All you knew of my mother was what you read from that small piece of paper my sister gave you, perhaps it's because she wasn't one of the God squad, who loved to let people see them putting paper money into the collection plate. You know, the ones you always seemed to give your special attention too." "How dare you!" he said. "No! How dare you, sir!" I responded, "Standing up on your pulpit, putting on an act of false condolence, who's going to absolve you, Priest?" That was the day religion and I parted company, I realised that you don't have to be a churchgoer to be a good person to talk to God.

Over the coming months, I was glad to be kept real busy working for Jackie, as it took my mind off missing my mother. I was surprised when some of the ladies who saw the results of their child's portrait, asked if I would come to their home and take a family group, which I was always glad to do, as it was more cash in the bank to enable me to set out on my own. I still had that burning ambition to be my own boss, so I contacted different companies who supplied all types of camera equipment, most of who would give you credit on a sell or return basis and, on hearing this, I was more confident than ever about trying to achieve what I had only dreamed about. I had made up my mind, it was now or never.

So over the next few weeks, when I wasn't working with Jackie, I searched for a small shop that I could lease and I was advised by another of my friends, who owned a paint company, to try for a shop in the vicinity where people would be prepared to spend money to get the best equipment for their hobby, so it was the case of pushing the boat out and getting as close to the city as possible, the rent may be a bit higher, but, hopefully, it would be a better catchment area for amateur photographers.

Another week had passed and my hopes were fading fast, that was until I began looking through the advertisements in the local paper, and there it was, just what I was looking for, a small shop to buy or lease and it couldn't have been better located in an area, which was about a mile from the City centre and was open to offers. Early the next morning, I called the 'phone number that was listed in the paper and made an appointment to see the premises.

That afternoon, I called at the shop address and was met by an agent from the renting company. The shop had previously been a confectionery, but the old couple who owned it were getting to the stage it was becoming a burden on them, so they were quite happy to get an income from leasing it or selling it. This was just what I had been looking for, it was not too small and had been kept in good condition, plus the fact and the shop had a bakery on one side and a post office on the other side.

40

On entering the shop for the first time, I noticed that everything that I needed was there; a large back room, where I could set up some seating and my equipment for taking photographs. There was a large window facing onto the street, this was ideal for to catch the eye of passing trade and this is where I would display cameras and the rest of the paraphernalia for anyone interested in photography. The shop had a good size counter and plenty of shelving, so the next thing on the agenda was to get a lease on the property and, when that was finalised, do some quick advertising. I had some flyers printed and gave the local postman a few pounds to deliver them on his round. Next were some business cards that would be placed on the shop counter, in the hope that any customer would take one and then they would have my phone number at hand.

Within two weeks, I was up and running and, although sales were a bit slow at first, over a short time, as people got to know where the shop was located, business really took off, especially at weekends when I was not only selling goods, but also being asked my advice about the best sort of camera to buy. I was still being asked to do some freelance work for Jackie, which would be mostly at night taking family groups at their home. I was quite happy to do this, as it was giving me the sort of bank balance that would help me further my business and outlets. I was now settling into my new surroundings, with all the new photographic stock neatly displayed on the shelving, in such a way that it would hopefully beckon the curiosity of potential buyers. Having gained a degree in my chosen profession and having hands-on experience working with Jackie, I now had two feathers in my cap, a heating engineer and a professional photographer. I was on my own now and quite confident, but I quickly realised that it was a case of stand or fall in this new and exciting challenge.

Fortunately, after a few months of the shop being open for business, the photographic enthusiasts of the local community were soon buying and even ordering all sorts of camera paraphernalia and I even got to stock a camera club which was on the verge of opening with brand new equipment.

41

Over the next three years, as the business flourished, it got to the stage that I realised I couldn't cope on my own and would eventually have to employ someone to assist when I was out on other assignments. The next day, I put a small advertisement in the local rag and was amazed at the response, I was inundated with all sorts of people, ranging from school leavers to older men who had just retired or, like me, had, unfortunately, been made redundant. It was a hard choice, but I finally settled for a young 18 year old disabled lad named Allan Kerr, who had lost his left hand in a car accident. I didn't choose him out of pity, but because he had an aura of confidence and appeared to be willing to learn, plus he also had a wonderful sense of humour. The day I interviewed him for the position, he told me how he had found it quite difficult to get employment due to his affliction, but when I explained to him what type of things that he would be required of him, most of all how to approach potential buyers, he responded by saying "Give me a chance and I'll have them eating out of my good hand." That did it for me, I hired him on the spot and I have never regretted it. True to his word, Allan was the perfect assistant, keen to learn and had a great rapport with all the regulars. Now I could go about my other side of the business, weddings, christenings and other small chores.

42

April 1972.

I still recall that afternoon vividly as it happened to be my 31st birthday the following day. Allan was out picking up our lunch and I was in the darkroom poring over some negatives that I was in the process of developing, when I heard the front door open, as the small bell above the doorway rang, informing me that someone had come in. I thought it was Allan, but, when I came to the front of the counter, my breath was drawn in sharply at the sight of the young lady standing there. She had the most beautiful serene smile, which complemented her green eyes, which appeared to sparkle as she spoke. I noticed that her complexion was void of any make-up, she was a natural beauty. "Good morning, how may I help you?" She appeared to blush slightly, and she seemed a bit nervous and unsure of herself, as she chewed on her bottom lip, before asking, "May I speak with the photographer please?" Drying my hands on a towel, I extended my right hand saying. "That's me, Martin Sinclair, photographer and owner of this establishment." As we shook hands, I couldn't take my eyes from her face, she had the look that one day would melt many a man's heart. As we broke off shaking hands, she seemed to gather some confidence before saying, "Mr. Sinclair, I'm looking for some advice. I would like the chance to have a modelling career, but the agency I approached asked me to have a portfolio of photographs taken, which they say will enhance the prospects of my being successful in this line of work."

It wasn't until she told me why she was needing herself photographed, that I gave her my full attention. She looked to me to be in her mid-twenties, quite tall with a statuesque posture that showed off every curve of her shapely figure. As far as I was concerned, she really had all that a top model could wish for. I asked her to take a seat in the corner and let her know that I would be closing the shop shortly, and, if she cared to wait while the last of my customers left, we could then spend some time over the many options that were open to her. She seemed quite happy with my suggestion, and then sat down.

As the last customer closed the door behind him, I brought another chair from the back room and sat facing her. "I think it will help if you begin by telling me your name." "Oh! Sorry, where are my manners? My name is Joanna Blair, but my dad calls me Jo, I think he would have preferred a son." "Well, he got a beautiful daughter instead," I replied "and I bet he's glad that he did. What type of modelling are you interested in Joanna? Fashion magazines, catalogues, catwalk etc.? There are so many choices to choose from, but I think I should warn you, everything isn't what you see in the movies, or the glamour models' photos in the newspapers. It can take years to get noticed and there are many pit falls and other matters of importance, which you shall have to decide upon before proceeding with a portfolio." She seemed to accept my revelations to what she may encounter, before saying that she wanted to carry on regardless of what I had just told her. "Look Joanna, I don't want you to make a rash decision, a portfolio can be quite expensive, so why don't you think about it over the weekend, and if you're still inclined to proceed, give me a call, my number and working hours are on the business card." As I opened the door to let her leave, she thanked me, before taking the card and putting it in her pocket, I then watched her walk down the street and in those few moments, I thought to myself that she had everything that was needed to be a success, at whatever type of modelling she chose. She had the look which complemented her perfectly curvaceous body, with a posture that oozed a sexual confidence that only a very few women are gifted with. Just at that moment Allan arrived back with our lunch." I noticed you getting an eyeful of that beauty who just passed me, wasn't she something?" "I did better than that laddie buck, I sat talking to her while you were out," "Well, I suppose that's one of the boss's perks, you're a lucky sod."

Just as we about to lock up for lunch, the telephone rang. That was all I needed, as the hunger pangs were beginning to creep in. I was caught in two minds, have lunch or lift the receiver? As I don't like to leave any calls unanswered, I decided to take the call and I'm so glad that I did. "Hello, Martin's photography," I was taken aback when I heard the voice on the other end of the 'phone." How's things Matey?" Here was an unexpected call from an old friend of the distant past. From the first moment I heard the word "matey" I knew who was on the line. "Pat Cairney, where have you been hiding all these years? You seemed to disappear to who knows where, so tell me how have you been?" "Well for a start, it wisnae to keep up with the Joneses, the whole family moved doon to Corby in England, as my faither's work moved there. He got better money and a better hoose, back and front door wi' a wee gairden. Everything was rosy, I had a driving joab wi' a removal firm, but my faither had tae retire, due tae his health, so we all moved up here again." "It's tremendous tae hear all that, but how did ye' get my 'phone number?" "It wis dead easy, Ah heard ye had opened a shop, so ah did ma Sheerluck Homes an' got yer number in the 'phone book. Martin, first things first, the reason ah'm callin', is tae see if you could possibly take some photies at mah mother an' faither's 65th weddin' anniversary. It's next Saturday night 7 o'clock in the St. Jude's Chapel hall. They don't know anything about what I am doing, as it's goin' tae be a surprise party. They think they're going to a church dance, so if ye' can manage, mum's the word." "Nothing wid gie me a greater pleasure Pat. I had a lot o' time for your mother, she was a fine woman. I'll be there about half past six and that gives me plenty o' time to get my camera's set up." "Thanks a million Martin, ah knew ye widnae let me down, so I'll see ye on the night."

How could I even think of refusing, it wasn't the first time that his mother helped out anyone in need? I myself would often go to her house to borrow a cup of sugar, or even some slices of bread, until my mother could get down to the shops for some groceries. I know for certain that many a child would be going to bed hungry, if it wasn't for the kindness of Pat's mum.

I closed the shop early on Saturday, enabling me to get to the Church in plenty of time, and to get a look at the hall where the anniversary party was about to be held. Also, it would give me time to get my equipment set up and ready for the happy occasion. As I was driving there, I began thinking back to the times when we were much younger and the things that the rest of the boys, who lived on our street, would get up to. One of our favourite games was getting hold of an old suit of jacket and trousers, stuff them with old rags and paper, wait in one of our friend's bedroom, which just happened to be three storeys high. Then, when we saw some girls coming up the street, drop the so-called body from the window, to hear the shrieks and yells, as the body crashed onto the pavement. Although, that came to an abrupt end, when a woman actually fainted and they had to call an ambulance, as she gashed her head when she fell.

One other occasion, which will live with me always, was the night that Pat and I were standing inside a shop doorway, sheltering from the rain, as we discussed what movie to go and see. We must have looked suspicious to the two policemen, who were passing by. They stopped to question us as to what we were up to. I began to explain to the one, who looked a lot older than the other officer, the reason we were standing there. The other policeman, who was a lot younger, took Pat aside, then suddenly, I saw him give Pat a hard smack on the face and heard him say, in a threatening sort of way, "Don't come the fly man wi' me son." At that, the one who was talking to me said, "Hey! That's enough!" to the one who had hit Pat, before telling us to move on and get to wherever we were going.

Once we walked away and further out of earshot, I asked Pat what the hell had just happened. He started laughing, as he told me when the copper who had been questioning him, asked if he had ever been in trouble, Pat answered by saying he was once in prison and when asked what for, he said he was there visiting his uncle and that's when he got a sore jaw. I thought there was no need for that sort of policing, perhaps the younger one was trying to impress his colleague, but was soon put in his place. Then it all came flooding back, this was the same Pat who coerced me into going to the dance where I first met Alexis. I thought I was over that sorry episode, but the wonderful times and the love that she showered on me, shall always haunt my memory. I'm glad that the Chapel hall came into view, as the last thing I needed to think of at that moment was how Alexis and I had spent a wonderful weekend together, as I knew it would only depress me in the same way, as it always did, whenever it crossed my mind.

As I walked into the Chapel hall, I could sense the happy atmosphere while I watched some women who, perhaps like me, had come early, busily placing some of the anniversary couples wedding photos and congratulation signs onto the walls, while others filled the buffet tables with all sorts of meats, sandwiches and soft drinks. After a short while, the hall began to fill as the guests arrived. By 7:30 pm, the dance floor was taking a real beating by the dancers, who were stomping their feet to a jazz tune that the small band were belting out. One of the men at the door gave an arranged signal, and just as Mr. Cairney and his wife came through the door, the dancers all stopped and stood applauding as the band began playing "Anniversary Waltz." I was in the perfect position to capture the look of sheer surprise on both their faces. When their maid of honour and best man walked from the crowd and handed Mrs. Cairney a large bouquet of roses, they were encircled by family and friends, offering their congratulations and good wishes.

There was a top table reserved for the special couple and their guests. I was sitting with a few of my old friends and their wives, as we sat recalling all the escapades we got up to, and some we couldn't mention, in front of the wives. While we sat talking about the old days, one of the women innocently asked me if I would ever get married, my reply to that was, "I haven't met a woman who would put up with me, and don't think I ever will, as I'm a bachelor by choice." Pat chimed in laughing, as he said, "Aye, by ladies choice, and don't believe him. What about thon cracker, ye were goin' oot wi', the wan frae the wee Cranhill social dance? All the boys thought ye' were hooked, ye' were inseparable." "That was a million years ago," I said, "it didn't go the distance." Thank God, that was the moment that the best man took the microphone and began his small speech. I didn't want that conversation to go any further. He then handed the mike to Pat's father who said, "I hope you all don't mind if I put my sentiments into a song," and, at that, he broke into a beautiful rendition of a Howard Keel song called "The girl that I marry, will have to be, as soft and as pink as a nursery." You could have heard a pin drop and, looking around, I could see women dabbing their eyes with their handkerchiefs. When he finished the song, he kissed his wife on the cheek and the applause was deafening. Then, the best man stood up and told the guests to raise their glasses to this wonderful couple. He ended his toast by saying.

"Here's tae us,
Wha's like us,
Gey few,
An' their aw deid "

That raised the roof, as everyone showed their approval, especially me, because it was a special toast my dear father gave after the Bells rang in the New Year.

I was kept busy going around all the tables taking photos, mostly of old neighbours that I had known down the years. I stopped at a table, at the far end of the hall and, just as I was about to take the photo, I thought I recognised one in the party. He wasn't one of my old friends, but he did look quite familiar. I knew I had seen him before, but where? I put it to the back of my mind, as it would now be the perfect way to end this wonderful night by having the whole company together for a large group photograph. Pat soon had them all gathered in an orderly fashion and, after the photo was taken, they all linked arms in a circle and sang "Auld Lang Syne," whooping it up at the top of their voices. After all the photographs had been taken and the goodnights and handshaking were over, the hall soon emptied, well nearly emptied, since Pat and some of my old pals carried on where we had left off earlier in the evening. Soon it became apparent that a few of them had over- indulged in the booze and would have stayed talking all night, if it were possible. But, just then, the hall-keeper, who was giving a helping hand to the bar staff by collecting the empty glasses, came over and said "Time to call it a night lads." It was time to vacate the hall, which was supposed to be closed by 11:30 PM.

43

I hurriedly began to get my equipment packed and was making my way to the door, when I felt a hand on my shoulder, "Hello Martin, it's been a long time since we last met, don't you remember me?" I was quite taken aback and, for the life of me, couldn't recall ever knowing who this was. "I'm sorry, but you have me at a disadvantage." "John McCabe. We worked with the same heating company, Moore's. I remember that you were made redundant, but they had to keep me on, as I was in the last year of my apprenticeship." "Yes! Now I remember. You were in the machine shop and I sometimes came and got some drills, or fan blades amongst other things. You've certainly changed, and for the better I might add, so what are you up to now?" "Well I'm here on holiday, staying with my sister, and I'll be here for a fortnight, but I'd like to have a chat with you before I go back to Jersey, would that be possible?" "Why not, but you should have come over to the table where I was sitting with some friends. Who are you with by the way?" "My sister works with Jean, the Cairney's oldest daughter, so she asked me to come with her, as she didn't want to come alone." "Would you like me to drive you both home?" "Thanks Martin, but my sister drove us here, so how do I get in touch with you?" I gave him my business card with the address on it and told him to call me and we could make some arrangement to meet up.

What happened the following week were the two things that, in a way, changed my life. On the Wednesday morning, I had a visit from the young girl, Joanna Blair, who looked lovely and had grown more alluring since the last time we had met. "Hello Martin, after taking your advice, I have given it a lot of thought and I would now like you to do my portfolio of photographs, which we discussed the last time we met. I need it for the model agency, who spoke to me about the terms and conditions of their contract. I think they are quite eager to have me sign, but I still would like a portfolio, as there is more than one agency out there." "Good thinking, Joanna, but I personally think you will have no trouble finding one." We agreed on a price and would begin the photo shoot the following Wednesday morning. Walking her to the door, I noticed that Allan had the look of "if only" in his eyes and he sounded tongue-tied as he called "bye" from behind the counter. Just as she left, the phone rang, Allan answered it before handing it to me, "It's for you Martin." "Hello, Martin here." It was John McCabe on the line. "Hi Martin, it's me John, I said I would call you for a get-together, so how does Tuesday night suit you? I thought we could go for a Chinese meal, or something else that you would prefer?" To be truthful, I had forgotten all about John, so not wanting to disappoint him, I said "Sure, why not, that sounds like a plan, where would you like to meet?" "Well seeing I've got the address of the shop, I could pick you up Tuesday night; say about 5:30 pm." "That's fine John, I'll see you then." Later, when I thought about it, I found it a bit strange that John and I had never really been workmates, or even worked together at any time, and yet, here we were about to meet and go out for a meal. I soon put it out of my head though, as there were some orders to catch up on.

The next day, knowing that I would be going out for a meal, I dressed a bit more formally than usual, as I was also going to the local registry office in the afternoon to take photos of a young couples' wedding. I got back to the shop around 5 o'clock and was about to take the rolls of films from my cameras, when John showed up. "Not too early, I hope?" "No, not at all John, just give me a few minutes to sort these films and we'll be on our way." "No rush, I've reserved a table at the Po San Chinese restaurant for 7:30 pm." I told Allan to lock up and I'd see him the next morning. "O.K. boss, enjoy the meal," then he started laughing as he said, "but, be careful what you do with the chopsticks, you could poke someone's eye out with those things."

As we drove along to the restaurant, I still had this nagging doubt in my mind, as to why he wanted to have this meeting with me. Walking into the restaurant, we were greeted by a small Asian girl, who led us to our table before asking if we would like something to drink before ordering a meal. John settled for a glass of Merlot, while I had a soft drink and, as we sat chatting while enjoying our drink, John placed his glass on the table and sat staring at the ice cube as he swirled it around. He appeared to be lost in thought, as though something was on his mind. Then, looking up from the glass said "Martin, I think now's a good time to put my cards on the table and let you hear the real reason I wanted to have a quiet chat with you."

Just as I thought, there's no such a thing as a free meal, so here's where the suspense ends. "I must begin by telling you that I have a very successful and prosperous heating business and have just been offered the contract to service every school and hospital in Jersey. This work shall last for years, the only drawback being, I can't get enough engineers to leave the mainland, so I've been approaching some of the men that we worked with previously. But most of them whom I approached were married with a family and didn't want to up sticks, because they had too many commitments here. Others were just happy to stay with their present lifestyle and didn't want to take the chance, at this stage in their life, as they were too set in their ways and didn't want to take the chance of things not being what they seemed. So far, I have drawn a blank. I realise that you have your own business, but I thought that we could come to some arrangement that would allow you to come over to Jersey and help out, by teaching some of my apprentices the skills that you worked so hard to acquire. However, you would be the tutor and would be paid top dollar, plus there would be no problem with accommodation, as I have a large house, with what they now call a granny flat which stands on its own and it can be yours rent-free."

What an offer! I must admit my mind was racing, I couldn't think straight. This was a complete bombshell that had landed on my lap. I eventually calmed down enough to answer his request. "I have to be honest with you John, that's a tremendous offer, and it really set me back on my heels, but you have to remember I have my photography business and my flat here. I also have a disabled lad, who has worked with me from the first day that I opened for business, what would the future hold for him? I couldn't just throw him onto the scrapheap, that's not my style." "Look Martin, you could at least sleep on it. I don't go back home for another week, we could meet up again and you can say 'Yeah or nay.' What have you got to lose?"

After we ate, he drove me home and we made another arrangement to meet at the same Restaurant, same time, the following Wednesday. Over the next few days, I was at a crossroad. My mind was in turmoil, as I weighed up the pros and cons of a situation that needed a quick answer. Here I was in my mid-40s, having worked as a high-rated photographer most of my working life. I began to wonder, was it worth taking a gamble on a new career path? Did I want to be taking photos and selling photography equipment for the rest of my days? Plus, there was a boom in the new digital camera market. These cameras were really becoming popular, because you didn't need a roll of film and you didn't have to get the photos developed. Also, they could shoot off 100 photos just by pressing a button, which meant it would soon get to the stage where all and sundry could be a photographer, as they could record things without any knowledge of a camera. This could be the end of the type of photography that was my bread and butter. Was John's offer too good an opportunity to pass up? The more I thought about it, the more I found myself thinking how humdrum my life had been over the past years. It was the same old, same old, every day. I knew I had a great bank balance, plus a very comfortable lifestyle, but no social life as such, mostly due to the fact that I had become more interested in working and making money. But, as the old adage says, "you can't take it with you!" I realised that I was in a rut, but if I accepted John's offer, this could be a new lease of life for me, after all, what did I have here? No friends as such to mention, only my young sister who kept in touch, and my older sisters who were both now married with their own lives to lead. All my time seemed to be taken up working in the shop, except when I was out doing weddings, and that meant working again. John had put a flea in my ear and I began to realise my life revolved around work and I was slowly becoming a recluse. Was this the right time to break some windows and let some fresh air into my life, before I was much older?

John came around as planned, on the Wednesday, and we returned to the same restaurant where we had dined the previous week. John appeared to be having a hard time keeping his suggestions in check and looked as though he wanted to get the meal over with as quick as possible. Once the meal was over and the table cleared, he ordered us both a Bacardi and coke. "Cheers Martin, I wish I could remember that toast that the best man gave at the Anniversary, it spoke volumes, but here's to us and what could be. Martin, I've taken the liberty of devising a plan that may sound audacious to you, but it could be food for thought. Let's surmise that, if it were possible, you could come to Jersey, to begin with and you could still have your photography business, leaving it in the capable hands of the young man, Allan, as you've taught him well, as far as I can see. Then, there's your flat to be taken care of, you could lease it out through a leasing agent, guaranteeing you a monthly rent. This means you would still have money coming in from your two properties, plus the fact that, if you agree to my plan, you automatically go onto my payroll. This means my company would be paying for your travel to Jersey and, as promised, you would have free accommodation. If things don't work out to your satisfaction, you still have your business and house here."

Even though I had previously given it some thought, I was still in a dilemma. I may never get another chance to try something new, as this sort of offer won't drop into my lap every day. Then again, I knew what I had here, was it worth taking a life-changing opportunity? "John, that's a wonderful offer and I'm nearly swayed to say yes, but it's come as such an unexpected surprise. I think I would like to sleep on it and give you a definite answer on Friday. If I agree to your terms, you'll realise that there would be a few loose ends to be taken care of here." "That's all I need to know, your word is good enough for me. So, until Friday then, I'll call into the shop around lunch time." On saying that, he shook my warmly by the hand, saying "No matter the outcome, I've found and gained a new friend."

As he drove me back to my flat, he gave me an insight on Jersey life. It was mostly occupied by French people and had a very busy tourist season all the year round, plus it was only a short air flight from the mainland and it boasted wonderful hotels, fine weather and great night life. It all sounded too good to be true, but I still had to weigh up the pros and cons. Over the next few days, there was only one thing on my mind, was I prepared to let this wonderful opportunity slip through my fingers? The more I thought about it, I soon realised I had nothing to lose and, looking at in the cold light of day, I was in a win/win situation.

On the Wednesday evening, I visited my young sister to give her a heads up on what I intended to do and asked her if she would mind keeping in contact with Allan, along with the leasing agency; she then would open a bank account for the monthly rent from the shop and the leasing agency, once my flat had been leased. She agreed at once and said she hoped that everything went well and made me promise I would keep in touch.

The following day, as we sat having lunch, I explained to Allan that I had this "once in a lifetime offer" from John, which I was going to accept and see what lay in store for me in Jersey. Upon hearing this, Allan was really taken by surprise. I knew, at once, what would be going through his mind, was he contemplating being told that he had no job? So, without delay, I told him that, if he wanted, I would like him to manage the shop in my absence, with a higher rate of pay, of course. The words were hardly out of my mouth before he quickly broke in on what I was about to say next, the look of surprise and the smile on his face, told me he was sold on my suggestion. "I'll give it my best shot and won't let you down." "Well, you're the boss now, Allan, and I'll give you all the backing you need, no matter what your decisions are, and when it comes to purchasing new stock, use your own initiative." I then told him of the arrangement that I had made with my sister, about how she would take the monthly takings, after he has taken his wages, and any outlay that had to be spent on equipment.

John showed up just after lunchtime on Friday and, upon hearing my decision, shook my hand warmly, "You won't regret this Martin, and I know you won't. I'm flying back to Jersey on Sunday, so call me at this number, once you have your flight arranged and I'll have someone pick you up from the airport. Martin, that's taken a weight off my shoulders and I shall not forget that. I'll have to rush off now as I have some things to get cleared up personally, before the week-end," and, on saying that, shook my hand once more saying "Thanks again, Martin."

44

As arranged, I phoned John at his office on the Tuesday, telling him that I would be arriving at the airport on Friday afternoon, giving him both my flight number and time of my arrival. On the Thursday, before leaving the shop, I gave Allan the address of where I could be contacted, in the event of him needing any advice from me. Then, I assured him I was only a few hours flight away, and not to hesitate to call me, if something serious arose. I also assured him he was in charge now and that I trusted him explicitly.

A cold and wet Friday afternoon found me at Glasgow Airport, where I had been sitting for the past five hours in the departure lounge. My flight was delayed, due to a fogbound Jersey Island. I was later informed that this was a regular occurrence and could last a full day. Fortunately for me, I only had to wait another couple of hours. I once heard it said that any travel that starts off badly always ends up being the best journey you'll ever know. I hoped there was some truth in that, as my immediate future was now in the lap of the gods.

When the plane touched down on Jersey, a cluster of tired passengers, including yours truly, meandered down the lifeless corridor towards the Customs. After clearing Customs, I made my way towards the large glass panelled revolving door and, upon stepping out of the Airport I was surprised by the weather. After leaving a rain-sodden Glasgow, I found myself looking at a cloudless sky and could feel the warm sun and fresh air wafting over my face.

It was so refreshing after the hours that were spent at Glasgow Airport.   I glanced up and down the sidewalk, when suddenly, a large black limousine pulled up beside me. It had black tinted windows, making it difficult to see inside. The passenger door opened slowly and, the first thing I noticed was a beautiful pair of legs, sheathed in four inch high stiletto heels, emerges from the car. I could tell that this person was physically fit, as those long legs were well-formed with trim ankles. Then an arm was extended, as if to beckon me to take hold of her hand, to assist her out of the limo. As I leaned forward to grasp her hand, I had my first look at this gorgeous creature. I had photographed lots of good-looking girls and women throughout the years, but this lady knocked the others out of the ballpark. She was strikingly beautiful and was wearing a pair of oversized Raybahn sunglasses. Taking my hand, as she emerged from the car, she stood and removed her glasses, before apologising for her tardiness. I couldn't take my eyes from her face. I thought I noticed a hint of a smile as she introduced herself, "Welcome to Jersey. I hope you had a nice flight, I'm Yvette, John's secretary and, as he's at another part of the island on a new project, I was asked to take you to his home and show you the layout of the house."

I was overwhelmed by this vision of loveliness and I seemed to be locked in a trance, as she struggled to withdraw her hand from my grasp. I was at a loss for words, but regained enough composure to introduce myself, "Thank you, I'm Martin and it's a pleasure to meet you." Her hair was deep auburn that bordered on red when the light shone on it. It was complementary to her eyes, which were a deep shade of green. The only word to describe her, adequately, was stunning. She also had the kind of plush lips men kiss in their dreams. Even with her incredible face, her body outshone it, although she wore a concealing outfit of loose slacks with a tight, figure-hugging jacket. I could only visualise her enticing statuesque figure, which was hidden from view.

Fast forward a few hours and, after arriving at the house and being shown around, Yvette shed her jacket on the chair.   I looked at this vision and my first thought of her would have made an angel blush. She interrupted my reverie, saying "You look a bit tired," then telling me to take a seat, as she walked towards a set of double doors on the wall. "This is what John refers to as his medicine cabinet." Upon opening the doors, I found myself looking at a stack of glass shelves, fully stocked with all sorts of liquor bottles. "Would you like a refreshment to help you relax after that gruelling trip? John won't be back for a few hours, as he still has to return to the office to pay out the staff wages." "I wouldn't say no to a Bacardi and coke, I think that should do the trick." I couldn't tear my eyes away her, as she poured out a good measure of rum. This woman oozed sexuality and a feeling of pure lust overtook me, as I watched her hips sway as she walked towards me. Even her footsteps on the wooden floor had a sexual rhythm. As she handed me the glass, our fingers touched, adding to what carnal thought were going through my mind.

As we sat talking, I found out that her mother and father was both French and they lived in St. Malo. Yvette also had lived there, until she got married. This marriage only lasted six years, culminating in a divorce. Now she was making a new life for herself in Jersey. I wanted to press her for more information, but she kept the conversation going by asking me had I left a family back home. She seemed surprised when I told her that my only family was my young sister. Then I continued sharing, with her, the rest of my background and my Photography shop and my flat.

As we sat enjoying our drinks and chatting about how life had treated us, out of the blue, she suddenly asked me "Were you ever married Martin?" I was taken aback by her question, but tried to make light of it, "No, I'm a bachelor, I was a slave to toil. There's an old saying back home, 'Engagement ring, wedding ring and then suffering'. So, I opted to stay single, just to be on the safe side." This caused her to throw her head back and laugh, "There may be some truth in that," she responded. At that, the phone rang, and as she walked over to the small table where the phone was resting, again I couldn't take my eyes off the graceful way her body moved. If I didn't know any better, looking at the motion of her swaying her hips, I could have sworn she was trying to tease me. As she placed the receiver to her ear, I overheard her say "Hello, yes, he's right here, hold on and I'll put you on to him." As she handed me the phone, she pointed to my empty glass and mimicked if I would like a re-fill, I nodded a yes and began talking to John.

It was the usual questions, after apologising for not being there to welcome me to the Island, he asked if it had been a good flight; how did I like my living quarters; and to make myself at home, until he saw me later.

After some more small talk and we had finished our drinks, Yvette suggested that if I felt up to it, she could give me a quick tour of the beach and the local shops, also the places I would be frequenting most. John's house was about twenty minutes from the beach, and my first view of it, stopped me in my tracks. The tide had ebbed out and I had never seen such a scenic view. It ran along the coast line, as far as the eye could see, the only blip on the horizon was the small harbour which was crowded by men and small boys fishing off the pier, while down below, all the fishing boats were spaced out, leaning at different angles on the dry sand banks waiting to be re-floated by the incoming tide. "What do you think of St. Brelades beach, Martin?" "I'm impressed, to say the least. It's magnificent; there must be hordes of tourists coming here for their vacation." "Yes," Yvette replied, "although sometimes it gets too busy, but, the islanders make their living from them and again, like everything else, some of the older residents resent being overcrowded, but, they have to take the good with the bad. Did you know that Jersey is also known as the Honeymoon Island, as it's famous for newlyweds to spend some time here?" "I can understand why, it's so peaceful and idyllic, a perfect place to get away from the hectic unending noise of the city." "Don't be too quick to judge," she responded, "the Island isn't what you would call family accommodating, there's nothing here for children, or even teenagers. For that matter, I believe they intend to keep it that way, which is a shame, for there's so much to offer." I thought that I detected a tinge of sadness in her voice and she appeared to frown, then suddenly, she was smiling again as she said, "I think we should make our way back, as John should be home any time now."

We just got in the door, when I heard the crunching sound of tyres coming to rest against the gravel on the driveway. As John came into the house and caught sight of me, his face lit up, then he rushed over and shook me warmly by the hand, greeting me like a long-lost brother. "It's great to have you here Martin. I hope you found everything to your liking. I know you'll settle in, once you get the feel of the place." "I don't think I'll have much trouble there, it's such a difference from the crowded city back home, everything seems so laid back here," was my response. "That's because the locals are all out working. But, it gets so much busier at the weekend, as the beach attracts all the younger crowds on Saturday, mostly to have a beach parties. However, it's much quieter on Sunday, as I assume they'll all be nursing their hangovers, after a hectic night. Now St. Helier's is a different kettle of fish, it's busy every day of the week, due to the fact it's the centre of the business fraternity, banks, insurance companies, solicitors and the local shops, which always appear to be crowded. However, you'll find this out for yourself, once you're accustomed to the Island." "I'm looking forward to that. Perhaps in my spare time, I will get to use my camera on the scenery that's on offer." "I know that you like Italian food, Martin, so let's all go out for a meal at the "Ristorante." It's a quaint, authentic little bistro and I have a feeling that you'll love what's on the menu."

"Now that sounds like a plan, I haven't eaten since this morning and, as I don't have a great appetite for food on a plane, my taste buds are already crying out for some Carbonara, or freshly cooked spaghetti." Yvette said, "I'll take a rain-check John, as I guess you both have things to discuss, so I'll have a nice relaxing few hours at home, watching some TV, with a nice glass of Pino Grigio to keep me company." In saying that, Yvette's parting words were "Nice to have met you, Martin. Enjoy your evening and I'll see you both on Monday." John walked her to the door, and she gave him a peck on the cheek as she said "Goodnight."

As Yvette drove away, John went over to the liquor cabinet and, as he was pouring out another few drinks, looked over his shoulder and asked, "So Martin, what do you think of Yvette?" "Well, she's certainly pleasing to the eye. I found her very amicable, in the short time that I've got to know her. She also struck me as being very confident, in an aloof sort of way." I replied. John responded, saying, "That's only a smoke screen, once you get more acquainted, you'll find she's a very humorous lady and educated to boot."

After finishing our drinks, we drove down to the "Ristorante Tivoli" and, as we entered, a young waiter approached us, but was quickly shooed away by a tall distinguished looking man, who, I later found out, was the owner. He grasped and shook John's hand "Buongiorno, Signor John, how are you? I haven't seen you for a while." "I've been very busy over the last few weeks, Alfredo, that's why I haven't had the chance to visit my favourite restaurant. Alfredo, this is Martin, a friend and a business colleague of mine. I told him that you serve the most wonderful Carbonara, so don't let me down." "For you Signor, it will be a gourmet's dream, or I'll have the Chef's head." We secured a table adjacent to a large window, which gave you the perfect panoramic view of the sea. As we sat down, the aroma that was coming from the kitchen made the hunger pangs begin to take their revenge, as though they were punishing me for not eating the meal that was served on the 'plane. It was a godsend that there were some breadsticks placed on the table, and nothing would have stood in my way of having one to eat, helping to suppress my hunger. The waiter came over with the menus and, without even bothering to look at it, I ordered the Carbonara. John opted for the Bolognese and asked for a parmesan cheese dressing. Returning with the cheese, the waiter then placed a small dish of pitted olives, garnished by oil and vinegar, in the centre of the table. How did he know this was a weakness of mine? Within a few minutes, I had cleared every olive from the small dish and was still chewing on the breadstick when our meal arrived. "You certainly put them away in record time, I knew you were hungry, Martin, but good Lord, when did you last eat?" "Around about half past seven last night, I didn't eat on the plane but, the Bacardi I had in the house helped stem the appetite, up until now." John laughed as he said, "I'm glad the waiter took the empty bowl away, or you might have had a go at that as well."

The meal was to die for. Then, Alfredo brought us over a carafe of his best house wine and sat with us for a short while. He was surprised upon hearing that I was from Glasgow and told us that he once lived there and how he remembered his father pedalling a tricycle, in the good weather, selling ice cream and frozen lollipops from the ice box that was fitted to a tricycle. He went on to tell us that his father eventually opened a small café in the East end of the city but, that all came to an abrupt halt when the war with Germany broke out and, as his whole family were Italian, they were interned in a camp on the Isle of Man, as were most families of Italian descent. When the war ended, his father opted to settle in Jersey. He opened another small café, which became very successful, because it was the only one there. I was 46 and married with a young family, when my father died." Alfredo concluded by saying, "So I took over the reins, gradually building it up, and now, gentlemen, you are sitting in the original café. Now, in a way, I have followed in my father's footsteps and have opened a small Bistro down by the waterfront." He then went on to tell us that his son, Giorgio, graduated with a degree in business studies, and a hospitality course in England. So, as a reward, he gifted him with the Bistro, for him to manage it in whatever way he chose.

After we said goodnight to Alfredo, we got a cab back home and ended the perfect evening with a few nightcaps, as we sat discussing how I would approach the workers on Monday morning. "Martin, I realise that, in a way, I'm throwing you into the deep-end, but I have every confidence in you and whatever you have in mind. I look upon you as the substitute foreman, and I want you to make your own decisions and get things done your way and you'll have my complete backing from the get-go." I pondered his words carefully before saying; "That's a lot of authority you're hanging on me, so let's hope your trust in me will prove you made the right decision." "That's what I wanted to hear, Martin. Now, I know you have had a rough day, so let's get some shuteye and I'll see you in the morning,"

It had been quite a tiring but eventful day and, when I entered my flat, I made straight for bed and, as soon as my head hit the pillow, I slept like a baby. As it was Saturday morning, I intended to have a long lie in bed, then shower before heading out to have a walkabout, making myself familiar with the district. Then I was in search for the new Bistro to have some breakfast. It was a beautiful day and I found it so exhilarating, as I journeyed down the cobbled streets and country lanes and, strange as it may seem, no matter where I ventured, the salty aroma of the sea filled my nostrils. I eventually came to a narrow thoroughfare, lined with shops on both sides, so with my hands dug deep in my trouser pockets, I strolled down the street like the lord of the manor, stopping every so often to spend a few minutes gazing into the shop windows. Most of which had the usual tourist gifts from the Channel Islands. I found that quite amusing to see the famous Mount Orgiel Castle in one of those little plastic globes that, when shaken, snow appears to fall. That was quite funny, for as far as I knew, it never snows in Jersey.

As it was early morning, most of the shops were still closed, but fortunately, the one that I was looking for, the small Bistro was already open and waiting to greet me. As I approached the shop, a youngish looking waiter was coming out the door carrying a wooden table, which he placed on the pavement. Then, returning inside, he came out with two chairs. Once again, he then went back into the shop and was about to bring another table out, as I walked in. He placed the table back on the floor, he bade me "Good morning, can I help you?" Good morning." I replied, "I was hoping I could have a strong black coffee and something to eat." "Certainly, I'll bring out the breakfast menu." In saying that, he went back into the shop and returned with the menu. As I perused what was on offer, I settled for a ciabatta roll with cheese, black coffee with a yoghurt to follow. As I put the menu on the table, he came back over. "Are you ready to order, Sir? "Yes, thank you." After telling him what I had chosen, I sat back and took in the wonderful panoramic view of the sea front. When he brought out the breakfast on a silver tray, he began placing the coffee and roll on the table and, as he was doing this, he asked if I was here on vacation and when I told him that I was here on business and that I had met his father the previous night. He smiled and told me that his dad had told him that John had visited the restaurant with a friend and spent a fine evening there. We sat talking for a short while, but I could see that the Bistro was becoming quite busy and, as there was only the girl, who was the Barista, serving behind the counter, I paid the bill. I then told him I would see him again next week and I began making my way home.

This was to become a regular Saturday morning ritual. It got to the stage where I could tell the comings and goings of some of the people, who resided near the Bistro. I would watch a young couple and their little girl, with her bucket and spade, stop at the florist to let the little girl smell the flowers, as they made their way to the beach to let her play on the sand. Then there was the elderly couple with their cocker spaniel dog, who was called Rusty, walking hand-in-hand on their way to the grocery store, with Rusty bringing up the rear. This was usually the time when the street would become quite busy with the younger crowd making for the beach, and the holiday makers who were out window-shopping.

On the way home, I stopped off and bought the local newspaper and once inside my flat, sat on the veranda to find out what was happening in my adopted hometown. I had scarcely read a few pages of the paper, when the phone rang. "Hello, who's calling?" "It's me Martin, John. I was wondering if you wouldn't mind going into St. Heliers' with Yvette, as she's taking a fair amount of payroll money to deposit in the bank. From there she will be going to hand over some cheques to a contracting firm, who have been doing some work for me. If you can manage, this will give you the chance to get a look around St. Heliers." "I'd be glad to ride shotgun, John. I've nothing planned, so it will let me get to know Yvette better." "You'll be lucky," he said. I was puzzled upon hearing this comment and, before I could ask him what he meant, he said, "Great, she'll pick you up around one o' clock and once she's been to the bank and contractors, you'll have the day all to yourselves." There was no way that I was going to turn John's request down. If truth be known, I was looking forward to this, it isn't every day you get the opportunity to spend time with such a beautiful woman as Yvette.

Just before 1:00 pm, I stood outside my door, head tilted upwards, letting the sun's rays beat down on my face. This surely was manna from Heaven, compared to the weather that I had left behind in Glasgow. Just then I saw the limo turn into John's driveway and, as I began walking towards the car, I didn't know what to expect but, was pleasantly surprised to hear her say "Hello again, it's good to have some male company for a change, it's usually one of the office girls who comes along." "Good afternoon, Yvette, I'm glad to hear that, as I'm looking forward to spending some time with you in St. Heliers." As I settled into the passenger seat, I couldn't help but notice that she was wearing her signature perfume and a red short pencil slim skirt, which stopped just above the knee; giving me the perfect view of her wonderfully toned tanned bare legs. Her white cotton blouse appeared to mould into every prominent curve, leaving nothing to my imagination. I felt like a tongue-tied teenager on his first date. I'm convinced she was getting a kick out of teasing me, when she lowered her head and peered over the rim of her sunglasses, looking deeply into my eyes, as she said "Are you ready to go?" "You lead and I'll follow," I replied. She then pushed her foot down on the clutch pedal, then put the car into first gear, causing her skirt to rise an inch higher on her thigh. Was she trying to see how I would react? Perhaps it was wishful thinking on my part but, I could have sworn there was a hint of a smile on her lips that seemed to say "Do you like what you see?" When I heard her sensuous voice, I began having thoughts would make a saint blush.

As we drove along the open country roads, she asked what I thought of the scenery. "Do you mean outside or inside?" There was no reaction, but I think she got the picture. We engaged in some small talk, as she wanted to know how I was settling into the job and could I ever picture myself living in Jersey. The strange thing was, she never spoke about herself and, if I asked her about her personal life, she quickly changed the subject. Was this what John was referring to when we spoke earlier?

It was around 2:00 pm when we arrived in St. Heliers. After spending another twenty minutes finding a parking space, we eventually made our way to the bank to deposit the cash, then it was off to the contractors to hand over the cheques for the renovation work being carried out on one of the buildings being completely overhauled, before new boilers and heaters were to be installed.

As we walked back to the car, I mentioned to Yvette what John had said, suggesting that I should take the chance of having a wander around the town. Now that I had the opportunity, I was going to do just that and she could take the car and drive home. When I'd finished seeing the sights, I would get a bus back to St. Brelades. "I don't mind staying here with you Martin, as it's been quite a while since I've been here. So, if you don't mind, I'll be your tour guide and, as we have all day and plenty of time to kill, we can both take advantage of this lovely weather." "That sounds great Yvette; however, I don't want you to think you are duty-bound to stay with me. I'm sure you have things to do and have your own plans for this afternoon." She responded, with a smile in her voice, "Listen silly, I would just be going back to my flat. Most of the day would be spent, like my usual weekends, lazing about in my garden, which I find pretty boring. Anyway, I like the idea of having something different to do, so let's go and do some exploring."

As we strolled along, exchanging small talk, I found her to be not only beautiful, but she also had a wonderful sense of humour, which is quite alien in most women. The clincher was when she told me that, as a young girl, she was a bit of a tomboy, always getting into scrapes. Like the time, when she was running down the stairs to get to the dinner table, after her mother had called her a few times, then halfway down the stairs, she tripped over a roller skate. The outcome was a broken middle finger and, when the hospital put splints around it, she walked about for weeks, with people thinking that she was giving them the finger. In saying that, she gave me a beaming smile. That smile had my thoughts jumping through hoops. The sightseeing was forgotten about, as far as I was concerned. Here was the real Yvette, giving me the insight of what lay beneath the aloof exterior that she showed as the professional private secretary.

We must have walked for nearly an hour, then I spotted a small café and, as luck would have it, there were a few empty tables. "Yvette, what say we sit for a while and grab a bite to eat, before I go on the drinking man's diet of no breakfast or lunch?" "Now, there's an idea," she replied. I ordered some meat and cheese sandwiches. It was amusing to watch the men giving Yvette the once over, wishing it was them sitting with this gorgeous woman.

"Tell me about your city of Glasgow, Martin. What are the people like, the culture and customs and what tourists and visitors find there when they come on holiday?" "Well, for a start, all men don't were kilts, only on special occasions, weddings or special events, like welcoming in the New Year. The majority of the people are very friendly to strangers and try to make them feel at home and, like all big cities, there's a plethora of fine architecture and museums, the difference being, that no matter what art gallery or museum you visit, it's free entry." "You make it sound so wonderful, you're very fortunate to have all these places to visit. Where I grew up in St. Malo, it didn't have much to offer, just like here in Jersey, interesting places were few and far between, and as for the night-life, it was more suited to the young people." I pondered her comments, stating, "Yvette, don't be fooled by the picture I'm painting, I live just 30 minutes away from Loch Lomond. This is a beautiful spot, where tourists, from all over the world, flock to. Yet, I can count on my one hand how many times I have been there. This is usually the case in most countries, where all these wonderful sights are at the population's fingertips, so what do they do? Instead of admiring what their own country has to offer, they travel to all different countries to see their treasures. So, in a way, they can't see the forest for the trees." "You're so right Martin, I never thought of it in that way, now I feel guilty of not going to see the Eiffel Tower." Again, there was that, 'I'm just pulling your leg' smile.

Soon, it was time to leave and, when we finished our meal, I stood up from my chair and waited for her to get up and, as she walked past, I placed my hand on her lower back to guide her to the door. "Is your hand going to stay there the whole way?" she murmured. I hesitated to answer but decided to leave my hand just as it was and pressed firmly, bringing her closer to me, "Yes, that's my plan," I replied with assertiveness, a wink and a smile. Her only response was a small winsome look.

As we walked along the boulevard, on our way to get the car, she locked her hand in mine and rested her head against my shoulder saying, "Martin, I must admit, I haven't had this much fun chatting with a man in a long time. Usually, all I got was polite chatter, or uninteresting stories. Perhaps, that's part of the reason I'm not too comfortable and wary of men." The rest of our conversation evades me now, as I just remember being drunk with a vague euphoria of being with this beautiful, charming woman.

As we got near to where she had parked the car, we stopped beside the picket fence of a small, whitewashed cottage and I told her I wanted to take a photo of her standing beside the fence. It was an idyllic scene, this stunning beauty surrounded by the background colour of the different shades of green that were adorning the trees. It was like the front cover of a fashion magazine. "You look every inch a model." I was being playful, but she really did. "You don't have to flatter me." "How can you flatter someone you can't stop thinking about?" was my response. When she heard this, a glimmer of a smile crossed her face once more.

As we drove home, she talked about her past and future goals. It was as though she was tapping into my thoughts by admitting that she couldn't envisage being committed again, and didn't hold any positive views of ever being married. I said that we were on the same page regarding that score as like her; I was career oriented and independent, wanting to live without any intrusions.   She dropped me off at my flat, thanked me once again for having such a lovely time, but there was a lot more I wanted to say to her. All I could think of saying was, "There must be lots of more interesting places for us to see and I know that you would be the perfect tour guide," "I'm sure I'd like that," she replied. "Perhaps when I come back from visiting my parents, we can get together again."   Upon saying that, she drove off and placed her arm out of the window, waving goodbye.

As it was now getting late, I decided to settle down for the night and chill out by watching some T.V. I mixed myself a drink. Sitting down, I began switching through all the different channels and finally ended up watching an old black and white war movie, but soon lost interest, as I began to think of the time spent with Yvette. Why was she so reluctant to talk about her past, why all the secrecy?

Sunday morning found me down at the small bistro, having my usual coffee and reading the local paper. Why I kept buying this paper, I'll never know. There was nothing in this paper that interested me, but I suppose it was better than sitting staring into space, but, help was near at hand. I was just about to ask for the bill when Franco came over with a glass of orange juice in his hand and sat down at the table. "Good morning, nice to see you again, I've been working at my father's restaurant for the past few days, as he was over in St. Milo, putting in his monthly order from his wine supplier. I opened the shop here, proceeding to go to the other restaurant, leaving the Barista and my other waiter here to run the show." "Well Franco, I suppose you won't be seeing me again until next weekend, as I shall be starting work at the factory tomorrow, so I'm using my last day of leisure to stroll around and follow my nose to wherever it takes me." "Could I suggest something to you?" he asked. "Certainly, I'm in no hurry, what do you have in mind?" He looked at his watch, before saying, "The morning church service shall be over very shortly, so don't take your eyes off that far corner at the end of the street." This sounded quite intriguing, so I did his bidding. After a few minutes, I could hear the melodic sound of the church bells, then voices approaching. As I watched the people reaching the corner, which Franco told me to watch, but, nothing was happening, as far as I could tell. Then, all of a sudden, two women came to the corner and one of the women let out a shriek, as the wind blew her dress up, exposing her underwear. It was like something out of an old time Charlie Chaplin film. She ran forward trying to pull her dress down and, as she tugged at one end, the front part of her dress ballooned upwards. I couldn't stifle the sounds of my laughter and people, who were passing by, must have got the impression that they were looking at a raving idiot. Franco must have heard me and when he came over to my table he too began laughing as he said, "The entertainment is free!" "You're a mischievous young man and a wily devil, Franco. Is this how you spend your spare time?" "Yes, but it gets better when the college girls come out for their lunch break. Many of the newcomers don't know what happens when the wind whips up, so I've seen some sights and some colourful thongs and panties. Let me tell you, some of them go commando, I've even seen what they wear under a burka." "At least now I know where not to wear my kilt," I said, as we shook hands and I took my leave.

After a walk along my favourite stretch of beach, I headed home and spent some time on the phone to my sister, to hear how she and her husband, Paul, were doing and how they were getting along. She told me that things couldn't be any better and said that she hoped to have some good news for me, when she called next week. So, what was the big surprise that she couldn't tell me? She also said that Allan was always prompt when bringing the takings, which were accumulating to quite a tidy sum and that he and Paul were becoming best of friends, going to football matches, whenever they had the time, and that was mostly weeknight games. I then phoned Allan at his house to find out how he was making out at the shop and the first thing he said was, "Martin, I took a chance on purchasing the few digital cameras. They were sold out within the first few days. I was getting a few inquiries from lots of people wanting to buy a digital camera, so I ordered around two dozen on a sell or return basis, but I shouldn't have bothered, as they were all sold within a fortnight. These cameras have really taken off and they're all the rage. They're so easy to carry around and produce great photos, so everything on this side is going great guns." We chatted for another twenty minutes or so, before I ended the call by telling him that I had made the correct decision by letting him use his initiative. I knew he had the makings of a top salesman. I then told him I would get in touch with him the next time I came home for a visit, hopefully, in the coming months. At that time, he could put me in the picture if he had any more ideas up his sleeve. It was getting late, so I showered then went to bed, thinking of what tomorrow would bring.

45

1976

As arranged earlier, I went up to John's house around 7:30 am. He was just finishing his breakfast and asked if I would like a coffee, or something to eat. "No thanks, I've already eaten, and the reason I'm here early is that I was hoping that you could give me a heads up before we went to factory." "I never thought of that Martin, but now's as good a time as any to give you the low-down on how things came to be.

Driving over to the plant, he explained to me, "There were no prospects on the horizon back home, as far as I was concerned, so I upped sticks and came over to Jersey. As luck would have it, I found a job with the McCann Heating and Plumbing Company. It was a small business and, after a few short years, I could see that the place was slowly dying, just like Mr McCann, whose health was deteriorating fast, due to the final stages of a terminal illness. There was a shortage of work, since no one was out canvassing for contracts. He had two sons, but none of them wanted to be involved in the plumbing business. One of them went to Kenya and had his own rubber plantation, and the other became a solicitor over in England somewhere. I found it shameful that he only got a yearly visit, if he was lucky, but that didn't stop him being proud of his boys and he would talk about them at every chance he got. It eventually came to the point that he was anxious to sell the company to get it off his hands. I could see that the factory had a future, if it could be organised properly. It was then that I approached Mr. McCann and put the proposition to him. I would be willing to buy the factory from him, if the price was suitable and the bank approved of my business plan. If I did get the bank's approval, it would give me the chance to keep the workforce, consisting of 12 plumbers; 4 semi-skilled labourers; 8 of whom were married men, in employment. He said that he would give it some thought. That was on the Tuesday and, on the Friday morning; he called me into his office to tell me that, if the bank agreed to my plan, I could have the factory for the amount we discussed. Saturday couldn't come quick enough. In fact, I think I was there before the Bank Manager. In a way, I was very fortunate, as I would normally have had to have an appointment but, as luck would have it, he agreed to see me.

My only worry was that I didn't have any collateral, but I wasn't asking for a real large loan. It was all down to what he thought of my business plan. Like Mr. McCann, he told me to leave my plan with him and he would get one of his auditors to see if it was viable, then he told me to come back to see him on the following Saturday. My hopes were once more in the lap of the god's. Now, all I could do was wait and try to stay positive for a good result. Let me tell you Martin, that this was the longest week of my life. All I could think of was what was going to take place on Saturday. One day would have me thinking everything would come up roses, then, other days would find me full of doubt. As you can now tell, I got the loan from the bank and I haven't looked back since. I now employ around 40 plumbing and heating engineers; 28 of whom are now doing a large contract job over in Guernsey; 15 semi-skilled labourers and 6 apprentices. As you know, I would like the apprentices to learn the trade, as fast as possible, to enable them to take the place of the men who are on their way to retirement."

Just then, we arrived at the factory gates and, as we drove through, John stopped at the gatehouse window and gave a short blast on the car horn. On hearing this, a small rotund man came out of the small gatehouse building and approached the car. "Good morning John, how are we today?" "Fine Albert, I want you to meet Martin, he'll be working here, so I'm showing him round the factory." "Pleased to meet you, Martin. I think you'll enjoy working here. "Thanks Albert, I know I shall." Just then another figure appeared from the gatehouse, only this time it was a giant of a man. He stood well over six feet tall and his build would have put a heavyweight boxer to shame. It was only when he got a bit closer, I noticed that he had a thin scar that started at his brow and ended at his lower jaw. He had granite features and looked to be in his early thirties, "Hello John, I haven't seen you for a while, where have you been hiding?" "Hi Vince, I was over in Guernsey on a business trip, so what do we owe to your visit?" "I came by to see dad and while I was here, change over the security tapes." "Oh! Sorry Martin, this is Vince, Albert's lad." "Hello Martin," he said extending his hand for a handshake. As we shook hands, I got the impression this man could break walnuts between his fingers and I was glad when he let go of my hand. "Well I'd better shove off," he said, "people to see and things to do, see you later, dad," and with the old tapes under his arm, he strode off. "Good God, John, that guy's a colossus." "Yeah, he's an ex-marine and has seen a lot of action, all over the globe. When he left the forces, he went into the security business. Now he runs his own company and supplies stewards for all sorts of events. His expertise is first-class. I've known him since he was young and before he joined the Marines. I spent a lot of time with him and his dad. Albert took me under his wing when I came to work here in Jersey. He was a great plumber and taught me quite a few tricks of the trade. Once I got to know him better, he could always tell when I was going through a bout of being homesick and he would often take me back to his house for supper. It was there I spent some time with him and Vince. He loved a game of chess, or dominoes, and many a night, we spent playing into the wee small hours. A few years after I bought this business, Albert was due to retire and, with Vince being away from home, the last thing I wanted was for him to spend his days sitting alone. In this way, he would always be busy and he would have all the other workers to talk with. After thinking long and hard on how to give him an interest in staying active, I offered him the job of doing some shift work in the gatehouse, by checking what materials were being delivered, or sent out to the different sites. He accepted my suggestion immediately and has worked in the gatehouse ever since."

After a short walk along a cobblestoned pathway, we came to a large corrugated shed that I took to be the Factory, "So this is where I'll be getting my hands dirty?" "I don't think you will Martin, that's the storeroom. Over here is where you'll be plying your trade." I turned around and followed his gaze and was taken aback by the three enormous, two storey buildings. "John, I didn't expect this, it speaks volumes for what you've achieved, as this is the perfect tale of the local boy makes good." "Martin, it didn't just happen overnight, I sweated blood to prove to myself I could do it. So, by having you here, I'm still making progress." He then showed me around all the different departments, beginning with the large storeroom and introduced me to the three workers, who were stocking up putting parts on shelves, then it was on to the tinsmiths, where they shaped and fitted the fan outlets, again I got to meet some of the workers. "You'll eventually get to meet the full workforce, Martin. Most of them go to the work sites straight from home, as it saves time by having them come to the factory, then going out on the job. I guess you'll still want to meet the apprentices. I'll make it a point to have them all here tomorrow, I'll get them all too assemble in the works' canteen."

We then moved into the office, where I was introduced to the secretaries, Betty and Pamela, who were both middle-aged. There was a younger girl, Beth, who was very petite and appeared to be approximately in her late twenties. However, she could have easily passed for an 18-year-old and very pleasing to the eye, especially when she looked up from her typewriter with her welcoming smile. We all chatted for a while, mostly about how I liked being in Jersey and the usual question that always seems to turn up "Don't you get homesick?" I got on their good side by replying "How could I get homesick, with three lovely ladies to talk with?" John laughed, saying, "Don't be fooled by this charmer, girls, he'll be much too busy to spend time giving you the low-down on what he gets up to."

With that, we both left, walking towards the canteen where we had a coffee and I made some plans for the next morning. "Since we've nothing more left for us to do here, Martin, you might as well go home. I'll see you tomorrow. I'd drive you back home to your flat, as I still have some things to attend to."

On my way out, I stopped off at the gatehouse and asked Albert to phone for a cab. While waiting for the cab to arrive, I found out that Albert was actually born in Aberdeen in Scotland. Albert was only four years old when his father, who was in the army, had to move the family to army quarters in England. Turning eighteen, Albert enlisted in the army at the outbreak of World War 1. He met and married a Jersey girl, whom he had met on holiday then, he re-enlisted in the Army, where he served for another fifteen years.

When he left the army, he found it quite difficult coming to terms being a civilian. After much thought of what the future had in store, his wife sold him on the idea of settling in Jersey, as she had been living there with her parents and convinced him that it would be an ideal place to set up home. He made up his mind and came to Jersey where he settled much better than he had expected.

Our conversation was cut short when the cab arrived, so I bade Albert goodnight and said I would return early next morning.

After being dropped off at the flat, I showered and went straight to bed. The next morning, I looked in on the gatehouse to see Albert, but he must have been out on one of his security rounds, so I headed to the canteen and waited for the apprentices to show up. Just before 8:00 am, they came into the canteen, between short intervals, until they were all present and seated. I introduced myself and told them the reason that I was here and that there would be no great changes to what they were already doing. The only difference being, they would all be shown how to weld properly; learn how to do sweat jointing; fit lead pipes to the fitted utilities, etc. More modern equipment would be installed, beginning with moving onto gas blowtorches instead of the old paraffin type, depending on what materials they would be working with. They would also be trained on how to use low pressure propane or butane gas, using a moleskin for wiping the joints. I then told them that I would be requiring a weekly record to see how they would perform sweating tasks on Brass Ferule joints, as this was an important part of plumbing work. I didn't want to appear to be too overbearing, since there was much more I wanted to find out about the way they were being taught, so I asked if there was anything that they would like to ask me. One of the older lads asked how they could be expected to learn some of the new work practises, while they were out assisting with the plumbers. I explained that, one by one, they would stay in the factory for part of the day, learning different aspects of plumbing and heating and that I would be there on an advisory capacity. They all seemed happy enough with my plan. Perhaps it was because they knew they would be away from the chores for a few hours. I thought to myself, if they thought this, then they were in for an unpleasant surprise.

Over the next couple of weeks' I could see the improvement in their work, as they seemed very keen to learn. Some of them struggled at the beginning, but after making them go through the same routine over and over until they eventually got the hang of what they were being taught, this gave both of us the satisfaction of knowing they had passed with flying colours. My only worry now was that they would try to impress the older plumbers with their newly found skills. For me, personally, it was great being back working with the tools again, and I looked forward of having the opportunity of getting my hands dirty by working on-site with the plumbers and also with the apprentices. It was a real eye-opener for me watching the heating engineers assembling the new type of modern fan heaters. These heaters were much lighter and more stylish than the ones that were fitted years ago. I soon developed a good working relationship with the men. I suppose they looked on me as just another worker and that was how I wanted it to be. Between working alongside the men, then taking time out to allow myself some teaching hours with the younger apprentices, my weekends couldn't come fast enough.

It had now become a habit of spending a few hours at my favourite haunt, Franco's Bistro, before taking my usual walk, weather permitting, along the beach. I would often make my way down to the sea front and sit watching the waves lapping against the shore, as the heady smell from the sea breezes wafted over my face, making it a joy to inhale the salty air. I always found it puzzling to see the flotsam that the waves left on the shore. I think I was on the verge of becoming a weekend beachcomber, picking up all sorts of unusual things, strange shaped seashells, or pieces of wood that set my imagination wondering how and where they had come from. I always felt that this was my comfort zone, bidding complete strangers a good morning, or watching the dog walkers setting their dogs free to cavort among the waves.

I looked at my watch; it was ten after two, time to make my way back home, as I wanted to stop by the factory to pick up some work sheets from the office. I had forgotten to take them with me the previous night. I buzzed the gatehouse and Albert came out and, upon seeing me, broke into his infectious grin, "Oh! It's you again, Mr. Sinclair, what can I do for you?" "Well, for a start you can start calling me Martin, I'd prefer that." "O.K. Sir." I think Albert forgot he's not in the army anymore. "I need to get into the office to get some documents which I forgot to take with me last night." "Sure thing, just let me get the keys, I was just about to have a coffee, so you're quite welcome to have one before you leave." "Sure, why not." I knew it would be good for him to have some company, as it must be boring sitting there with no one to talk with.

When we got back to the bothy, Albert poured the coffee. As we sat, I asked him about his Army days. He began by telling me all the places where he had served and some of the things that he and his mates got up to. My favourite story was hearing how, when he was stationed in a small border town in France, one of the boys made a trip to the local brothel, only to be sent packing by the Madam, after being told Scottish soldiers were not welcome there. When asked why the reason for this, she retorted "Wee Jocks, big cocks, no money." When I heard this, I spluttered on my coffee and nearly choked laughing. It was getting late and I was truly sorry having to leave Albert and the rest of his tales, but I'm quite sure there would be other times.

I arrived back home around 4:00 PM and tossed the documents, which I had taken from the office, onto the table, and decided to have a quick shower before settling down for the night. This gave me the chance to peruse over the paperwork which some local contracting companies had forwarded for tendering approval. I was just on the verge of pouring myself a small Bacardi before heading for the shower, when the telephone rang. "Hello," but before I could say another word, I recognised my young sister's voice. She sounded so excited as I heard her say, "Hello Martin, it's me, Anne. I thought you would like to know that you're going to be an Uncle." "That's fantastic," I replied, "congratulations, that's the best bit of news I've heard in months, I know that you'll make a wonderful mother and how's Paul reacting, now that he's about to become a dad?" "To be honest Martin, he's getting on my nerves the way that he fusses all over me, he won't even let me make a cup of tea, I think he expects me to sit around all day and not move a muscle." "Hey! Don't knock it, "I said, "I thought that was what all new expectant fathers do?" "Yes, maybe in the movies, but that's for the happy endings. I won't let it happen to me, I'm quite content doing my housework, as it keeps me busy and helps to pass the time away." "Well, you know best, and when's the baby due?" "According to the doctor sometime about November, give or take a few weeks, so I guess it will be around Xmas time" "Just make sure that my name is on top of the Christening list." "You know that's a given, especially as we want you to be the Godfather." "I'll, be proud to be there, come rain or shine." I could picture her smiling at my response, then she said, "Martin, I'll have to go now, but I'll keep you up-to-date on what's happening, Allan will be up sometime this week with the shop takings, so take care and stay safe." "Thanks Sis, I'll call you next week and, congratulations once again." I missed her wedding, as they didn't want the hassle and opted for a civil ceremony. One thing was for certain, I may have missed her wedding, but there was no way I was going to miss the christening.

Between the heavy workload and the few hours spent with the apprentices, I finally made it through the punishing week and I was literally dead on my feet. Now it was a case of having a shower, getting the paperwork done, then straight to bed. I certainly didn't need any rocking to put me to sleep, even though it was just 10 o' clock.

I awoke on Sunday to a rainstorm and perhaps that set the tone for the day. I felt so lethargic, it was as though all my vitality had ebbed away and even the thought of making myself something to eat was a chore. My full day was spent moping around the house and, to make things even worse, the television channels offered no respite, as each channel was as bad as the one before. It got to the stage where my entertainment was watching the rain bouncing off the street, or the rivulets of rain that were splashing against the windowpane making zig zag patterns as they raced to reach the bottom first. I began to remember how, at one time, I dreaded the thought of Monday mornings, as that was the start of my working week, now here I was ready to welcome tomorrow morning with open arms.

The first thing I did, on my way to the factory, was to drop in at the florists to purchase a gift box of Jersey carnations and had them forwarded to Anne, along with a congratulations card. I had just left the florists, when the Heavens opened once more; causing the rain to come down with a vengeance and here I was, caught in the open, as the deluge showed no mercy to man or beast. That settles it; I thought to myself, I must get a car as soon as possible. To make matters worse, having to make a run to the factory, I realised how unfit I was. Once inside the office, I virtually sank into one of the secretarial chairs, wheezing and coughing, as I fought for air. "If you're trying to catch the 'flu, you're going the right way about it!" I turned around in the chair, and I was surprised to see Beth, the young attractive secretary. "Just look at the mess you're making on the floor," she commented. Looking down, I could see the small puddle of water surrounding my feet. "Would you like me to put on a hot drink, a tea or coffee, to try and get you warmed up?" When I heard that, I realised I was soaked through and began to feel myself shiver. "No thanks dear, I think my best idea is to get back home for a change of clothes and, on the way there, I'll buy myself an umbrella, so, if anyone calls, tell them I'll return their call as soon as possible."

As the rain was still drumming on the street, I called for a cab and, once home, had a quick hot shower and that seemed to do the trick. On returning to the factory, I was told that one of the apprentices was waiting to see me in the office. It was one of the younger boys, John Irvine. As I came into the office, he stood up with his head bowed, looking at the floor. "Sit down, John, what can I do for you?" "I don't know where to start, Sir. I really like my job, but I don't seem to be grasping what you're trying to teach, I see the other lads making progress, but I feel like a failure and I'm thinking of looking for another job." I looked at this despondent young man, "Wait a minute John; you're doing alright, as far as I can see. You can forget the idea that you're a failure; the only real failure is the failure to try that bit harder, so no more of that kind of talk. I'll always be here to help, that's my job. If you have a problem, let me know. Now get back to work and remember what I told you." "Thanks boss, that's what I'll do." He left my office, with his shoulders pulled back, hopefully having gained some confidence by what I had told him. I sat waiting in the office, expecting the phone call from one of the contractors. We found that this contractor was always reliable by the way in which his tradesmen always got the job finished on schedule.

At that moment, I suddenly remembered that I was badly in need of a car, now that the winter months would soon be here, the only problem was I didn't know any car dealers, so it would be a matter of getting some advice and the first thing that came to mind was to ask John. The phone call eventually came and, when I finished the conversation, went back to the paperwork that had been sitting on the desk over the weekend. On the way home, I stopped off at John's house, but as usual, the house was empty, where does this guy get to? I've not laid eyes on him for the past few weeks. I suppose he's out wheeling and dealing, but I guess this is the price you pay for keeping the business successful.

As I left the house the following day, I was greeted by another cold blast of wind, followed by a heavy burst of rain. That settled it, I thought, my mind was made up – I must invest in a car. As I reached the warmth of the office, I saw Beth chatting with a co-worker and they both smiled at me when I came in, "Good morning, Martin. By the way, we received another telephone call from Yvette informing us that she would be returning this weekend, as her father made a quick recovery." This was music to my ears, as I suddenly realised how much I missed her. Approaching Beth, I asked her if she could let me know where I could inquire about leasing a car. She flashed me one of her lovely smiles and said, "You are in luck, my husband just received a new company car and his other car is sitting in the driveway. If you prefer, I'll have him call you." By the end of the day, it was all settled, now I had a car. With the weekend approaching, I found myself eagerly anticipating Yvette's arrival. I inquired when her flight was coming in from St. Malo, now I could pick her up when she arrived.

Saturday morning found me at the airport. Finding a seat close by at the Arrival Terminal, I relaxed my nerves with a cup of coffee. Time seemed to crawl by, when I suddenly caught a glimpse of her coming through the gate. The surprised look on her face brought a smile to mine. She immediately rushed forward and, before I knew it, she gave me an unexpected warm embrace which made me feel wanted.

As I drove her home to her flat, we arranged to have dinner that evening. Yvette suggested the La Belle Ma Maison restaurant, which was renowned for pairing their famous wines with their gourmet entrees and appetizers. Once seated at the table in the restaurant, our conversation was pleasant, but stilted. This confused me somewhat, but I quickly brushed that feeling aside, as I looked at her beautiful face. We shared a tremendous evening and when she suggested that I stop by her apartment for a nightcap, I was euphoric. Once inside her flat, I helped remove her coat and, as we settled down on the couch, I let my arm drape over the back of her shoulders. Looking deeply into my eyes, she said, "Martin, I have some good news and some bad news." I sensed, with some trepidation, what she was going to tell me, so I said, "Give me the goods news first, Yvette." "The good news is that I just received a letter from my ex-husband's solicitor, advising I would be getting full custody of our son, as he was planning a new life in America with his new wife." This came as surprise, as I never knew she was once married and had a young son. Now came the bad news. Her eyes seemed to fill with tears, as she said, "I will be going back home to St. Malo, very soon, to be with my son and take care of my father, who both need me." This was the worst news I had heard in a long time, more so when she said, "If only we had met a few years ago, Martin, things would have been a lot different." Upon saying that, Yvette threw her arms around my neck and we clung together, as though our very lives depended on it. I began to remove the pins from her hair, freeing the tresses from their confines to cascade over her shoulder. With each stroke of my hands on her hair, each curl undone and each ringlet freed, she sighed a soft feminine moan, as her arms encircled my torso, she then pressed her cheek to my heart. For a while, we sat like this, before she extracted herself from my embrace, stood up before unbuttoning her skirt, letting it fall to the floor, before stepping out from the skirt puddle at her feet. She then began to unbutton her blouse until she was standing only in her underwear. I felt as though I was in a dream. She was wearing a full set of the sexiest underwear, all white and virginal from the gossamer see-through bra to the white suspender belt and the pair of silk panties. My heartbeat had quickened, as I watched her remove her bra and thong, and it felt as though it was ready to explode. Looking into her eyes, I reached out my hand and traced my fingertips along her lips, and she responded by kissing them playfully. I took in her delicate chin, her slender neck, noting how it pulsated each time she swallowed, as she lulled her body to stillness, submitting to my inspection. My gaze took in the curvature of her shoulders and the gentle protrusion of her collar bone. Forcing myself not to hurry, I followed the soft sloping of her chest, until my eyes settled upon the most beautiful breasts that I ever had ever seen. They were shapely rounded and swayed naturally; her nipples adorned the pinkness of her areola and were akin to large cherries that stood erect, as she moved towards me. The full creamy mounds of flesh, undulated with every ragged breath she took, and each crowned with those prominent peaks of her globes which strained upwards as though begging for my oral attention. I was mesmerised and I couldn't restrain myself from whispering, hoarsely, "You are so beautiful." She moaned lightly at my reverential tone, and her thighs twitched involuntarily and this small movement caught my attention, causing me to tear my eyes away from her proud nipples, to travel down her body. I drank in the soft curves of her stomach, her tapered waist and the wide child-bearing hips that had invaded my thoughts since our first encounter. And there, at the apex of her ample thighs peeking out from beneath a thatch of well-tended silken curls, were her lower lips, the essence of her femininity and the entrance to her untold treasures. I could see that she was now a seething and tempestuous cauldron of sexual hunger, and it would be cruel to deny her any longer. From the first contact of her soft, pliable lips against mine, I knew that I had to have her. As I pressed myself against her, my tongue darted between her lips, seeking entry into her mouth, only to find that her tongue had a similar goal to my own. We kissed passionately, as we both knew that this would be our last time together. I took her shapely nipple between my teeth, before paying homage to the other nipple, then running my tongue along and down her cleavage, causing her to moan with pleasure. Our unbridled passion was punctuated only by her soft sighs, and sounds.

I knew that this was the moment that I had often envisaged. I was mesmerised and felt that my shaft was about to explode. I wanted this tremendous feeling to last forever, but I couldn't wait any longer and now was the perfect moment to remove her panties. As I moved her to the edge of the couch, she lifted her hips as I slipped her panties down her thighs. I then spread her legs to let me nuzzle close to her mound, She had a delightful womanly scent and as I pressed my face against her labia, I could see the dark curls that were covering her love channel and, on opening the entrance to her treasures, I could see her swollen clitoris peeping out from its hood and, as I touched it with the tip of my tongue, she pushed her open thighs towards my mouth arched her back and cried out like a banshee as I entered her with my tongue. I realised she was now at the point of no return, so I placed her on the edge of the large sofa to allow me to part her thighs with my fingers, allowing me to penetrate her love grotto, which was now slick with her love fluids.

This caused her to pull me closer, before softly whispering into my ear, "Please make love to me now." No words could ever convey what it felt like to have my full length buried deep and up to the hilt, as she kept moving her body in rhythm with every stroke that I thrust into her. When we both were on the verge of exploding, she wrapped her legs around my waist to pull me in deeper and after we had both reached the pinnacle and shared my seed, we lay ensconced in each other's arms.

The silence spoke volumes of the sadness that we shared at this moment. We should have been rejoicing in what we had found but, instead, realised this was the end of a beautiful in our life. Time seemed to pass slowly, but we both knew the inevitable had to happen. I arose from the sofa, reached out for my clothes, got dressed and looked into her eyes for the last time, as we both realised that the dream was over.

As I drove back to my apartment, there was a feeling of emptiness which could not be shaken off. However, knowing that time was a great healer, I hoped that this unsuspecting disappointment would not fade into oblivion and I consoled myself by remembering that I would always have the memory of the fantastic evening of sheer bliss that had been afforded me by Yvette.

46

As the months passed, albeit ever so slowly, try as I might to remember, the memory of that night with Yvette gradually faded and I finally banished them from my thoughts. A feeling of foreboding was like a shadow that followed me wherever I went. My only answer was to throw myself wholly into my work. This helped in a way, but it was now October, with winter fast approaching. The weather was becoming cold and dark and the sun was surrendering to the cloudy skies. The holiday atmosphere faded and this, in turn, curtailed my evening walks and got to the stage where the only option open to me was to hope for a few weekends of better weather conditions to give me the chance of getting out of the flat. The walls of my apartment seemed to be closing in on me and it was becoming a lonely haven, interrupted only by the occasional hours of flicking through the television channels, until it was time for bed. Every night was the same pattern, but that was soon to change after John phoned me one afternoon to let me know he needed to speak with me urgently and could I meet him at his home around 7:00 pm that night.

When I arrived at John's home later that evening, the moment I entered the house, I knew something ominous was about to happen when John's first words were, "Martin, have a drink. Sorry to have you come over at this time, but something has come up that requires immediate attention. As you know, we have a large project in Guernsey and Robert Smith, our foreman, who is the only one capable of reading the plans for the new heating system, has become ill and had to return to the mainland and knowing that you have similar knowledge of reading the drawings, I was hoping that you could fill in for a couple of weeks, until John is on the mend again." I thought to myself, this was surely a godsend, because it would take my mind off other matters. I responded, "Glad to help out, John. When would you like me to leave? " The relief on John's face was palpable and he broke into a big smile, saying, "As soon as possible Martin, I really owe you big time, I'll call ahead and arrange for you to stay at the same small hotel where Robert was staying, it's called the "Bellway" and it belongs to the lady who manages it, her name is Mrs. Fontaine and, as far as I know, by talking to Robert, her husband was French but she's English so there should be no language barrier. Martin, call this phone number when you arrive in Guernsey and I'll have one of the works' plumbers pick you up and take you to the hotel, then next day take you to the work site."

After arriving home, I just stepped through the door of my flat, as the phone began to ring. "Hello, who's… "But before I could say another word, the voice at the other end asked if I was Martin? When I answered in the affirmative, he said he was sorry to have to interrupt me at this time of night but he was the other security guard and thought that I should know that Albert was taken to hospital after being assaulted at the factory. He went on to say he had gone looking for Albert, as it was time to change shifts, and when he found Albert slumped at the back door of one of the sheds, where they keep the scrap lead, he called for an ambulance. After thanking him for giving me a heads up on the situation, I made my way to the hospital. As I got to the ward where Albert had been taken, his son, Vince, was walking up and down outside the room where Albert had been taken. "Hello Vince, how is Albert doing?" "I spoke to him for a few minutes before he was sedated, but he managed to tell me he noticed that the guy who struck him had a tattoo of a snake on his wrist. I am waiting to see the Doctor," he replied "to find out how serious his injuries are." "Has anyone contacted the Police yet? "I asked. "The Police won't be involved." Vince blurted out. "But what about the Insurance Company, they'll have to be told?" Vince turned and faced me and I could see the anger on his face, as he spat out, "Fuck the Police and the Insurance, I'll be handling the situation myself. In fact, this conversation never took place," Just then, the doctor arrived with some x-ray negatives. Turning to Vince he said "Your father has a fractured jaw and badly bruised collar bone, so he'll be staying here for observations over the next few days. You may as well go home now, as you won't be seeing him tonight." "Thanks doctor, for keeping me in the picture. I'll see you later Martin and thanks for your concern."

It must have been around two in the morning when I arrived back home. It had been a very long day, so it was straight to bed, knowing that the first thing I had to do in the morning was to make a booking on the Concord ferry for the first sailing to Guernsey, to me this would be a welcome change of scenery.

It was now the middle of October and when I arrived at the dockside, I noticed that the sea was rather choppy. I stepped aboard the gang plank, leading up to the first deck of the ferry. I soon realised that choosing to make the journey by boat, was a bad move. Even though the ship was anchored, I could feel it rocking, as the waves dashed against the hull. "Ahoy there." Upon turning to my left, I found this small gentleman at my side. At first glance, I thought he was one of the crew, and then on closer inspection, I noticed that he was wearing what I thought to be a naval cap, as it had an embroidered anchor on it, instead, it was one of those crass caps that you can buy on holiday. I must admit though, he did look the part, with his dark blazer, white flannels and plimsolls, not forgetting the silk cravat that he was wearing with his open necked shirt. "Looking forward to the sail, young man?" "I'm afraid not," I replied, "I'm the original landlubber with a preference for rowing boats on a calm lake." "Not me," he said "I love sailing in any weather conditions. Well, I'd better push off and see if my better half has ordered something to eat as we missed breakfast." "That's it," I thought to myself, "don't just stick in the knife, and twist it."

This was the longest three hours I had ever spent. I sat the whole journey with my eyes closed, hoping to shake off the nausea, but my insides were heaving more than the ferry. At last, we had finally made it and, as my fellow travellers and I made our way gingerly down the small gangplank, who should I find in front of me, but Hornblower himself. He looked as though he had been pulled through a hedge backwards, ashen faced and his hair all tousled, the cravat was halfway around his neck, as for the cap that he was wearing, I guess that went overboard with his breakfast. I just had to ask "Well, how did you enjoy the trip?" He replied in a voice, which was barely audible, "Fuck that for a carry on, we'll be flying home at the end of our holiday."

It was such a relief to be back on terra firma. I could still feel the effects from the endurance that had caused me to go weak at the knees. I found it a struggle walking and having to carry my suitcase, so I sat on one of the bollards to let my stomach settle, before slowly making my way from the dockside. My next move was to find a place where I could phone and contact the factory. The ideal solution was to locate a bar or restaurant and, from there, kill two birds with one stone, as I was in desperate need of a strong black coffee, then afterwards I could phone the factory and get picked up, just as John suggested.

After a short walk, I came across a small bistro "The Tivoli." I placed my order, and then I sat outside to get some fresh air, hoping to ease the queasy feeling in the pit of my stomach. When the barista placed the cup on the small table, I couldn't get it to my mouth fast enough. From the first sip, the dark brown nectar was, for that moment, the best cup of coffee that I had ever tasted. Finishing the coffee, I used the number that John had given me and called the Factory. "Good afternoon, McCann's Heating Company, how can I be of assistance?" "I'm Mr. Sinclair and I'm inside the "Tivoli" bistro down by the harbour and I was told to call and one of the workmen would pick me up." "Certainly Mr. Sinclair, I've been expecting your call. I'll have one of the drivers come and collect you right away." "Thank you, I'm much obliged."

47

Before returning to my table and ordering another coffee, I bought the local newspaper from a circular rack, which also happened to be filled with postcards, mostly showing the usual places to visit. There were others with panoramic scenes of the local beauty spots, castles, beaches and different views of the local annual flower parade. As I scanned the postcards, I was surprised to see a card showing the house of the world's renowned author, Victor Hugo. This man was one of my favourite authors since the first moment I had to read some of his book "The Man Who Laughed" as part of a school English exam. Ever since then, I was hooked, but even though I had read most of his books, I never knew that he had once lived on Guernsey, one of the Channel Islands, but at that very moment, I knew that I just had to visit the house of this genius. As I stood at the counter paying for the few cards that I had bought to send home to my young sister, a young man dressed in a blue coverall approached me, "Mr. Sinclair?" "Correct, I guess you must be here to drive me to the factory, would you like to stay for a tea or coffee?" "Thanks, I'd love to, but I still have some piping to deliver and unload at the site. I'm Jim Bell, by the way, labourer and driver and, after all these years, I've got to know the Island like the back of my hand, so if the time ever comes that you want to see any part of the Island, I'll be happy to take you there." "That sounds good to me, Jim. By the way, just as a point of interest, how did you and the men address Robert Smith?" "We just called him Bob, as that's what he liked to be called." "Good, as far as I'm concerned nothing's changed, I want to be called Martin from now on" "Sounds good Mr.,,, sorry, Martin." "Before we go to the site Jim, I'd like to drop off my luggage at the hotel, and on the way there, you can give me a head's up on what to expect. John gave me the name of the Hotel but, I've forgotten the rest of what he told me." "Well I think you'll find the Hotel to your liking. The woman who owns and manages the Hotel is Mrs. Jessica Fontaine. She has a daughter, Tracy, who assists in the running of the Hotel and is married to the Chef and, by the way Bob spoke, he said the place was first class, especially the food. You'll be the only member of the workers who'll be staying there, the rest of the boys stay in cheaper "digs," as most of them are family men, sending home money to their wives at the end of each month. You're roughly about a fifteen minutes' walk from the Hotel to the school that we're upgrading. At the moment, my main task is to get to the site early and open the large Porto cabins where all the heating materials are stored. Since I have to be there early, I take the trailer home at night, so when the weather's bad, I can pick you up and drop you off at the school, that's the arrangement I had with Bob." "Thanks Jim, but I'll be leasing a car for the weeks or months I'll be here, but I'd be obliged if you can pick me up Friday, say at around 7.30 am, as I want to have a look around, while it's still quiet."

After a short drive, we found ourselves outside my new abode. "I'll see you in the morning Jim and thanks again for the lift." As I carried my suitcases up the gravelled path leading to the front door, I noticed a few cars parked on the forecourt that told me that there must be other guests staying here, so at least I'll have some company in the evenings. Just as I got to the front door, it opened and I found myself looking at a very attractive woman, whom I would guess, would be in her middle fifties. "Hello, I saw you coming up the path, I've been expecting you, I'm Jessica Fontaine, but most folk call me Jess, which I don't mind as it is less formal, especially for the guests." "Hello, I'm Martin Sinclair and I'm very pleased to meet you, Jess," "I'll get Tracy, she's my daughter, to show you to your room, then perhaps you can have something to eat." "Thanks, but a shower will suffice, as I couldn't eat a thing after that boat journey, I'm afraid I'm a dry land sailor." "Yes, it can be a rough crossing. Perhaps later, you'll feel like having a light supper." She then got Tracy to show me to my room, which I found to be to my liking, very spacious with a large bed and two wardrobes which faced the small sink that had a large mirror and medicine cabinet just above the wash-hand basin. Tracey was a very sweet and friendly girl and, as she was about to leave, she said "I hope you enjoy your stay in Guernsey, I think you'll like it here and, if you need information on anything or places of interest, timetables etc. don't be afraid to ask." "Thanks Tracey, that's good to know, as I'm looking forward to exploring the Island. "

Once I unpacked, I made my way down to the small lounge and found Jess talking to one of the other guests. When she saw me, she excused herself from her conversation, came over and asked if I would like something to drink? I opted for a gin and tonic, before Jess introduced me to some of the other guests. There was a Welsh couple named Dower and a couple from Derby, whose name I just can't remember. In fact, I only ever saw them at breakfast as they sat together at the table, and sometimes at night where I would find them playing cards or Baccarat, they were not the most talkative people you could encounter. Jess told me they came to her hotel every year to spend Xmas and New Year. I personally think they were hibernating in case they had to talk to other people and happy to stay indoors and play games. The next morning, after an early continental breakfast of croissant, yoghurt and black coffee, I waited for Jim to pick me up. I had just finished eating, then hearing the sound of Jim's car horn; I thanked Jess for the lovely breakfast and left the Hotel to meet Jim. As I got into the van, I said "Let's get to the site Jim, as I want to have a look around, and for a start you can tell me how many plumbers are working on the site at present." "Around about 30, Martin, but as you probably know, they all have specific jobs to do and I think you'll find they're a good bunch of lads. Maybe I shouldn't be saying this, but there's one exception, Paul Strang. He's a lazy sod and he's the biggest lead swinger on God's green Earth. He walks about most of the time trying to look busy, sometimes carrying a bit of material on his shoulder, or old drawing plans under his arm, but try catching him working is a complete waste of time. He's great at delegating though, giving out instructions, providing he doesn't have to take part with what's to be done. The only reason I'm telling you this is I don't think it's right that he leaves all the work to other people and gets away Scot free. You'll also find that there are no apprentices on this site, only fully qualified engineers." Thank God for that, was my first thought, I don't have to nurse apprentices anymore.

When we got to the site, I checked out the office, then began inspecting how the job was coming along, checking out all the different rooms and found it a real eye-opener to see that the most up-to-date heaters had been installed, along with the newest of air vents, so everything seemed to be well in hand. As it was now late Wednesday afternoon, I'm glad that I decided to wait until Friday morning before meeting the workers, as I was still feeling a bit out of sorts, so it was straight back to the Hotel and an early night in bed.

Friday morning found me back at the site and the first thing I noticed was what looked like a huge garden shed. Later that day, I found that this was constructed to be used as an office and security gatehouse, where the security guard would keep a check on the materials that were coming and going. As I strolled around the site, some of the men, who were going to start their day's work, passed me by, giving me some quizzical looks as they must have wondered who I was. I waited around until the full work force of the men were all doing their specific jobs, before making myself known. As Jim had said, they looked a good bunch of lads and, as I approached them, one by one, speaking to them, I found that they knew all there was to know about heating.

Over the next few days, I remained in the office with the woman called Betty, who was a temporary secretary. She told me that she was working here presently and, once this project was finished, she would be placed by her company at another job. A few weeks passed and I was now settled in, but one afternoon, I was having a look around to see how things were coming along, when I noticed a piece of trunking which was used to hide the electric wires from view, and helping to make it look tidy and the finished article. Just at that moment, who should appear with his usual old drawing plans tucked under his arm, it was the man himself, Paul Strang, "Who are you?" I asked, knowing full well who he was. "I'm one of the heating crew and I'm on my way to install a heater vent." "Well I'm your new foreman and I'm not happy with that piece of loose trunking, so get it fixed." "Alright, as soon as I finish what I'm doing." "Good, well see that you do," was my curt response.

Over the weekend, I leased a small car. As it was early Saturday morning, I decided to visit the house where Victor Hugo had lived. Although I was using a map of the Island, I had to stop a few times to ask the directions to the house. When I eventually arrived, I felt I was on hallowed ground, as I made my way to the entrance of the house. There wasn't another soul in sight, except for the curator, who looked so old and feeble. When he saw me, his face lit up as though I was the prodigal son arriving home. "Bonjour, and good day to you. I welcome you and hope you have a good visit to Victor's house." "Thank you, I know I will, as I have been an admirer of this genius for many years, from boy to man." "Come then, let me show you the small chair and table where he wrote 'The Hunchback of Notre Dame' and the 'Toilers of the Sea.' His original quill pen is still lying on the table, along with a book that he kept notes in." He then went on to tell me how he was exiled from France in the year 1855 for his political views and lived in Guernsey for 15 years and how it took all that time to write "Les Miserables." Here I was, looking at the table where a genius sat composing a story that would eventually run as a musical in London continuously since 1985 and has been considered one of the greatest pieces of literature of all time. The old curator certainly knew the history of Hauteville House, where the author spent most of his time writing his books, but I wasn't finished just yet, as he took me outside to the garden to show me the oak tree that Victor Hugo personally planted and is still flourishing to this day. It was now time for me to leave, but before leaving, I handed the old man 20 pounds and told him it was worth every penny to have what seemed like a personal tour, along with his knowledge of the main happenings in Victor Hugo's private life.

On my return to the Hotel, I made straight for the lounge, ordered a Bacardi and coke and sat at the fireside and began browsing through the local newspaper. It was all the typical mundane articles that didn't, in any way, interest me, until one story caught my attention in a way that had my mind racing, it was an appeal from the Jersey Police asking for any information on a man that was taken to hospital. It appears that he had been found lying severely beaten in a shop doorway and had been in a coma since arriving at the hospital. They described him as being in his late twenties with a tattoo of a snake around his wrist, then a contact number of the police office. It seemed that Vince had wreaked vengeance on his father's abuser, but as the man said, "What goes around, comes around." In a way, I felt sorry for the guy in hospital, but remembering how old Albert looked, justice seemed to have been done.

Monday was such a fine morning, I decided to walk to the site, instead of driving, mainly because of the wonderful breezes coming in from the sea always put a spring in my step and made me feel so fresh. I met a few of the men heading for the job that they were doing, so it was a good morning all round. I had come to know most of them now and found it easy to mingle with them. Later, I did my usual walk around the site to see how things were progressing. When I walked through the door of one of the rooms, the first thing to catch my eye was the electrical trunking that I told Strang to fix. It was the exact way it was left the other day. I did an about turn and made for all the other rooms, until I came across him. He was standing below the trestle of an engineer, who was drilling the wall to take one of the heaters. As I approached him, he must have seen me coming and began to walk away, "Just a minute," I said when I caught up with him, "come with me." We walked in silence, until we came to the room with the loose trunking, "I thought I told you to get that sorted." "I was busy," he replied. "Well get it done now!" I spat out, "OK, I'll get one of the men to get it right away." "No you won't. I'm telling you to get it sorted NOW, I'll be back in an hour, so there will be hell to pay if it's not finished and, by the way, I'll be keeping you busy from now on." By the look on his face I could see the anger in his eyes and the veins on his forehead appeared to be throbbing, as if ready to explode. "This is downright harassment," he suddenly spluttered. "No, but you can take it as a verbal warning from your foreman," I replied, "and the next time I find you slacking off, it will be a written warning and after that it's hit the road Jack." On saying that, I left and made my way to the office where I could check the mail and try to get in contact with a contractor whom I had spoken to some weeks ago, concerning new fixings that we were waiting to be delivered.

When I arrived at the office, Betty told me she had left a note on my desk, I thought that it might be from the contractor, but when I responded the next morning, it was Bob who answered. "Hello, I'm Martin Sinclair. I'm the guy who's been acting as their foreman until you return back to work." "Good morning Martin, Bob Smith here. John had already told me you would make sure everything ran efficiently while I was gone and I hope that you enjoyed having the break in Guernsey and found the Hotel to your liking. I wanted to let you know that I'll be coming back over on Friday the 18th and hope that we can meet up and you can give me a rundown on what's been happening since I've been away." "I'll be more than glad to see you Bob and, if you tell me what time you'll be arriving, I'll pick you up from the airport, I'll be the one standing with a book in my hand." "Thanks, I'll certainly do that Martin, so I'll see you then." The minute I heard the date that he was coming back, I called the airport and made a booking for the first flight out to Jersey on the Monday morning and began looking forward to returning to the comforts of being in my own flat.

Bob called back the next day and informed me he would be arriving around 11 o'clock, so my last three days would be spent getting prepared for my departure. That evening, after supper, I called Jess aside to give her the news that I would be leaving on Monday, as Bob was coming back to take over as foreman once again. I gathered that he would be taking the room that I would be vacating. Jess said that she would be sorry to see me go, but told me there would always be a place for me in her Hotel. That same evening, I got a 'phone call from Paul, telling me that Anne had delivered a baby daughter, and both were doing well. The moment I heard that, I called John and told him that, after putting Bob in the picture, concerning the situation at home, I was thinking of going home for a week or two. John's response was "By all means Martin, you have certainly earned a holiday and I hope you have a great time with your family and I'll see you when you come back."

As planned, I met Bob at the airport and as we drove to the Hotel. I gave him a heads up on how the work was progressing and was well on schedule. I told him I was leaving for Glasgow on Monday afternoon on the 3 o'clock flight and asked if Jim could drive me to the airport, as I would be returning my leased car on Saturday. "No problem Martin, I'll see to that right away and make sure Jim will be there to drive you."

When we got to the Hotel, Jess gave Bob a welcoming hug and said his room was all prepared for him. After supper, we sat in the lounge relaxing with a drink. It was a wonderful change to have someone to talk to and it gave me a chance to put Bob in the picture. The next day I took the leased car back, before taking a stroll down to the beach to take some photographs that would remind me of the many times I had sat on the sea wall admiring the view, watching the fishing boats land their catch and the young boys and grown men fishing from the pier.

48

That night, I packed my suitcase and was ready for my departure from Guernsey. I then made my way to the kitchen to say my goodbyes to Tracy and her husband and thank them for the many wonderful meals that were always served with a smile and a "Bon appetit."

Early on Monday morning, I made my way to the florists and selected two beautiful bouquets of roses, one for Jess and the other for Tracy, and then I surprised them by presenting the flowers to them after breakfast. It was heartening to see the look on their faces, as I thanked them once again for the way in which they made me feel right at home. Jim arrived to pick me up at 2 o'clock, and Jess and Tracy walked me to the door before each giving me a hug wishing me "Bon voyage" and telling me to send a postcard from Glasgow.

When we arrived at the airport, I handed Jim two bottles of malt whisky to give a drink to the men on site, thanking them for making my job easy and trouble-free. "They'll appreciate that Martin, as you were a fine foreman and treated everyone with the same respect. All the best Boss, and thanks again."

Once inside the airport, I found a seat in the bar next to the departure lounge and ordered a Bacardi and coke to unwind. I had not given it much thought over the past months, but I guess, more than anything else, I felt a bit empty and lonely at the Hotel, but now I was looking forward to getting home and seeing my sister and the new baby. The bartender was busy drying glasses when he looked at me and said "Whoa, check her out man, she's a real hottie!" I looked up to see who he was talking about. I saw this vision walking past and she stopped a few yards from where I was sitting, before bending down to get something from the small valise she was carrying. Even a blind man could see that she had a gorgeous figure and, as she stood up with her phone in her hand, I watched as she searched her phone for something. It was then I noticed her face. It was not what you would call cute or sexy, it was simply haunting, in a Grace Kelly sort of way, a classic beauty that had an angelic look. As she looked up, I noticed that her eyes were an amazing shade of green, which I found intriguing. I couldn't take my eyes off her and felt the urge to go over and talk to her, but chided myself, thinking it would be awkward to approach a stranger in such a manner. I decided it would be best to sit watching her with a sense of excitement that I had not felt in a long time. Suddenly, an elderly lady, who was using a cane and limping very slowly, stumbled and fell to the ground and her purse flew open scattering the contents all over the floor beside the girl, who did not pause to help her to her feet and assess if she was hurt. I realized that I should help, but more than that, this was the perfect opportunity to meet her.

As I ran up to them, the girl was leaning over the old woman who appeared to be a bit dazed, "Is she alright? "I asked, as we helped her to her feet. "I think so," smiled the angel, "She's a bit shocked more than anything else." "Oh! My goodness, I have no idea what happened," the elderly woman panted." "It's alright, we'll get you right as rain again," and, in saying that, the girl looked up at me, smiled and gave me a quick wink. Her voice was soft and gentle and had a melodic tone which complemented her beautiful face, she continued to reassure the woman that she wasn't hurt, and no harm had been done.   We both slid our arms under each of hers and guided her to a seat, several feet away, then we went back to retrieve the belongings from her purse. "You're so sweet to help, thank you," she smiled, as we began to pick up Kleenex tissues and coins that were scattered all over the ground then placing everything in the old lady's purse. "My pleasure, of course, what kind of person would not help a lady in distress?" I smiled back at her, "Plenty, unfortunately," as she gestured to people speedily walking past us, oblivious to the incident as they raced to the departure gates.

As we walked the lady to the departure gates, I heard the young lady say some reassuring things to the old lady about how we all take a tumble from time to time. The woman confessed her embarrassment over her fall. I soon realised that in a few minutes we would be boarding the plane and the 'angel of mercy' would be making for her destination and, unfortunately, I might never get a chance to see her again and wondered what I could say to connect with her. Just as we said our goodbyes, the girl turned to me, smiling," Well, thanks again for your help, and it only proves that chivalry isn't dead." "Think nothing of it. I was only too glad to be of assistance." As she turned and began walking towards the check in gate, she called back, "Thanks again Martin, it was nice to meet you again." "Wait, you know who I am?" I asked, desperate to make her turn around. "Sure, you haven't changed a bit since you did a set of wonderful photographs for my portfolio. I'm Joanna Blair and I remember, as if it was yesterday, when I came into your studio, quite unsure of myself and you put me at ease by giving me such sound advice on my modelling career." "Thanks, that's good to hear, you've certainly changed and, if you don't mind me saying so, you look like a million dollars. I could put you in the bank and live off the interest. So, where are you headed?" I was desperate not to let this young woman out of my sight, without knowing more about her. "Glasgow," was her quick response. "You're going to Glasgow?" I interrupted. "Yes, I've just arrived in from the United States to meet some family and friends. I now live in the U.S. and have a modelling business there. In fact, one of the models, who works for me, came over to Glasgow with her fiancé and his mother last week. Her fiancé's mother is also Scottish. She hadn't been back on home soil for more than twenty five years. Just like me, she was born in

Glasgow and settled in America. When I heard they were coming to Glasgow, I made up my mind that I should take a break. So, here I am and, before we left to come here, we made an arrangement to meet up at the Hilton hotel, where I'll also be staying for ten days before going back home. It was really a nice coincidence to have met you again Martin, but if I don't hurry I'll be late for my flight."   I quickly responded saying, "I think we're on the same flight and, if you like, we can walk to the departure gate together."

The ten minutes waiting at the gate, gave me a chance to have a quick chat and glean some information on what she'd be doing during her vacation and, before I knew it, they were calling out my row number. I was elated knowing that we would be travelling on the same flight and began mumbling to her about perhaps seeing her on the 'plane after boarding. She told me that we were ready to board. Once we had walked down the tube and onto the 'plane, we began looking for our seat numbers and she paused in front of her seat number and lifted her carry-on over her head and placed it in the overhead bin above her seat. Once more, the gods smiled on me, and I found that I was sitting on the aisle seat right beside her. As she sat down and began fumbling with her seat belt, I noticed that her skirt had slid up, exposing her shapely legs. Part of her skirt fabric was caught on the side of her seat and was pulling up just enough for me to see that she was wearing a garter belt that was holding up her silky nylons. Now, any man out there will tell you, that there is something insanely sexy about a woman who wears garter belts, but a woman as beautiful as she was, wearing them was literally making me drool. As she adjusted her seat belt, she must have noticed, because she pulled her skirt down, which was probably a good thing I didn't want her to see me ogling at her. We began chatting about how the course of our lives had changed in so many different ways. She asked me if I had ever married and was quite surprised when I shook my head and briefly told her the reason that it wouldn't be right to ask a wife to stay at home, while I would mostly be away working on various projects. As if to prove a point, I gave her a good example of how I had been working and living in Jersey, then Guernsey as a favour by helping out a friend, but I was getting bored living out of a suitcase. She, in turn, said that she had modelled for about five years, adding that what I told her all those years ago about becoming a model was not all bright and glitzy, just as I had predicted. In fact, the jealousy and bad feelings amongst some of the girls was hard to believe and it got to the stage where she wanted to get out of the business as fast as she could. Now, she ran her own modelling agency, making sure all the girls worked in a pleasant atmosphere and there would be no vying for positions. She then told me that she had been married for three years, but divorced shortly after. Prior to the divorce, she wanted to give up her business and settle down and have children, but her husband said he was not ready to be tied down. This caused arguments and resentment because she wanted to be a mother. However, he was adamant that nothing I said would change his mind, so there was going to be only one outcome – divorce.

I could see the forlorn look of sadness in her eyes as she explained this sad episode to me. Suddenly, she changed the subject by asking about what I did in my spare time and she could see that I was excited as she was, to be going back home for a few weeks. She was so warm and sincere, making me feel so comfortable to be with her and I found myself telling her more about my life, more than I had shared with some of my best friends. All too soon, it seemed that we had just got on the 'plane, when the Captain's voice came over the speaker saying we were about to land. As we touched down, I said our best idea was to let the hordes rush to get out, as we had plenty of time to collect our luggage. While waiting at the carousel watching out for our luggage, I realized I had to see her again, so I told her I would like to spend some time together over a meal and look back on old times. "Yes," she replied "that would be lovely, but Friday night is out, as I have another invitation from my friend to have dinner at her Hotel. She and her husband married last year but, due to him sitting his final exams, they had to forego going on a honeymoon, so they opted to come to Scotland and celebrate here. In fact, why don't you accompany me there, as I'm sure they would love to meet a true Scotsman?" "I'll go for that," I answered, "sounds good to me." "Martin, before we meet up again, I think that it's only fair to let you know that I have a partner back home, she was a tower of strength when I was going through the depths of confusion and depression of my break-up." "This doesn't change a thing," I replied, "Now; I have a new friend who still means so much to me." We arranged to meet at 7 o'clock on the Wednesday night at her friend's Hotel, so that we could still have a few drinks and reminisce over old times.

The next day I visited my sister to see the new baby and to find out when the baby would be christened. It so happened that it would be on Wednesday after the morning Mass, so that suited me, as I could spend the morning at my sister's, go home later and get suited up for to meet Joanna. When I finished my visit with my sister, she showed me the bank book where she had placed all the weekly takings from the camera shop. and I was staggered by the amount of money that had accumulated over the year.

The next day, I popped into the shop to see Alan and was surprised at the difference he and Paul had made. They had transformed the place, bringing it right up-to-date and were now selling DVDs, as well as the most current camera equipment and they were in the process of selling i-Phones which were selling like hot cakes. "Allan, I told you to do what you thought best, as you were now in complete charge and I can see I made the right decision." "Thanks for giving me that chance Martin, and I know it can get even better." Before I left, I reiterated how impressed I was and told him to give both he and Paul a 15 per cent rise for all the hard work that they had put into the shop. I was feeling buoyed by all that had taken place on Wednesday, seeing my sister, my new niece and how successful the Camera Shop had become, and now I was elated at the thought of having dinner with my friend Joanna and her friends from abroad. I returned to my hotel, where I was situated temporarily, as my flat was on lease to a tenant, I had a hot shower and proceeded to get all dressed up for the upcoming dinner. It had been a long time since I felt this good about myself; it seemed as if all my concerns were washed away by the hot water cascading down my back.

When I arrived at their hotel, I was ushered into the restaurant and saw Joanna and her friends already seated at the table. There was a young woman and a tall, dark and handsome young man sitting there, and it was the man's face that looked so familiar to me. Had we met before? How could that be? He was supposed to have just arrived from the States, as you could tell by the overall tan he was sporting and that "American look" about him. Joanna introduced me to him, saying "How curious, you both have the same first name. Martin, this is my friend, Marty and his new wife, Melanie." As I shook Melanie's hand, I couldn't help but notice the brooch she was wearing, I thought to myself, where had I seen this brooch before? Then it suddenly dawned on me, I was looking at the Topaz Butterfly. So, my mother's prediction was coming true – the butterfly will always come back home! I shook off my reverie, and faced the young man being introduced to me. I shook his hand and told him I was delighted to meet him and his new bride. He had a firm handshake, and said, "My mother will be down shortly, she had been unpacking her suitcase and it took her longer to get ready." At that, he glanced up and said, "Here she comes, a day late and a dollar short." Of course, this was meant in a jovial manner. As I looked up, my blood froze. I was shocked to the core, could this be who I thought it was? This vision came walking down the staircase, a tall, statuesque beauty with short silver hair, but the face had not changed....it was my Alexis!!!! Good God, what was going on? I felt my knees shake, and I was at a loss for words. Marty touched my elbow, asking, "Martin, you look like you have seen a ghost. Can I be of assistance?" I looked at him, then looked back at the lady coming down the stairs and said, "Is this your mother?" "Of course," he responded. I stood up, my chair tumbling backwards and excused myself quickly, as I headed for the bathroom.

I thought I was going to pass out. Here was this couple, the young bride wearing the Topaz Butterfly on her dress, the young man who, in my mind, was a mirror image of me....and this mirage of a person resembling my Alexis, descending the stairs.... was I losing my mind? My shock turned to anger, I needed to get to the bottom of this, and fast. I splashed cold water on my face, and then I headed back to the table. As Marty stood up to introduce his mother to me, I interrupted him. "I need no introduction, young man, I know your mother, and she knows me." I looked at Alexis, who was sitting down with her head in her hands, and I noticed there were tears running down her face. Joanna was perplexed at what had transpired and was looking for an explanation. I asked Marty if I could have a few minutes alone with his mother and he quietly acquiesced, and I proceeded to usher Alexis to a quiet corner of the hotel. As we sat at a small table in the foyer, I felt an uneasiness envelop me, not knowing where to begin. All I could say to her, "What in God's name happened to us, Alexis?" She was silent for a minute, then she lifted her face to me and said, "Martin, it will take a long time to explain to you what happened, and this is not the time, nor the place to do so. Could we possibly arrange to meet somewhere later, so I can explain fully to you and then to Marty? I know this is a shock to you, but he is your son."

As I heard the words, "......he is your son," I felt the air being sucked out of my body, and words escaped me. What was she saying? My son, MY son......I looked into the anguished eyes of the woman I had loved all my life, but, at this moment, felt nothing but anger towards her. I took a deep breath, then managed to nod my head, saying, "Yes, but I want to meet with you alone, we'll meet at my hotel, tomorrow morning at 10:00 am." At that, I scribbled the address on the back of one of my business cards, turned and marched out of the restaurant. As I stepped onto the sidewalk, I gulped in the cool air, trying to clear my head. Everything was played over and over in my mind. So much had evolved over the last hour or so......my precious love, Alexis, had returned, looking just as I remembered her so many years ago and, now, she tells me I am the father of her son! I hailed a taxi to take me to the hotel, and once there try and clear my head, which I felt was about to burst.

Upon entering my hotel room, I called room service and ordered a bottle of Johnnie Walker whiskey. Slumping down on the sofa, I sipped the drink slowly, closing my eyes, ruminating all that had taken place over the last couple of hours. I began wondering what would be revealed to me when Alexis came to my hotel room.... I was prepared for the worst, but hoped for what would turn out to be the best solution. The rest of the day was spent going over my past, trying to make sense of all that had taken place. I thought it best to keep an open mind, but secretly, I was excited at the prospect of seeing Alexis again and hearing what she had to say, but I knew I had to stay calm until all was revealed to me.

The day passed slowly, and I wished I had taken Alexis by the hand and dragged her to my hotel to hear what she had to say. However, I knew it needed time to take all this information in and listen, before coming to any sort of conclusion. After drinking most of the bottle, I finally went to bed, tossing and turning most of the night, unable to escape into a deep sleep, hoping to escape all the machinations running through my mind.

At last it was morning. After dragging myself out of bed, stumbled over to the coffee pot and poured a cup for of strong black coffee, as my head felt there was some gremlin in there with a jack-hammer, causing me to squeeze my eyes shut to alleviate the pain of this hangover. The coffee did help; I began to tidy up the room before having a shower, then wait for the visit from Alexis. Promptly at 10 am, the phone rang. It was a message from the front desk saying that I had a visitor. My heart was thumping so hard, I could hear it echo in my ears, what was I going to say to her? If I was honest with myself, I felt like clutching her in my arms, wanting to never let her go, but I knew I had to listen to what she had to tell me. Going down to the front lobby, there she was, my love, my life, my everything, standing before me. Looking intently into her eyes, I detected there was a sadness, a deep sadness that I had never seen before, but suddenly my anger bubbled up in my chest as I realized so many, many wasted years had passed and now, all of a sudden, Alexis was going to explain to me what had transpired. I took Alexis by her arm, and guided her to the elevator, saying, "Let's go to my room, Alexis."

49

As I ushered her into the warmth of the room, I pulled a chair out for her to take a seat and asked if she wanted a coffee. As she sat down, she looked up at me. "Martin, please don't be angry with me, but believe me, when you left for England, I waited every day for your letter giving me your new address. Days and weeks passed, and I kept asking my mother if there was any mail. It was always the same answer, no mail for me. Into the bargain, she was becoming sarcastic over the weeks and said she was growing tired of me asking her if there was mail, smirking as she told me not to hold onto my dreams, telling me he was never going to contact me. I even went to your old address and was told that all the people had been relocated into new housing schemes, which were built up on the outskirts of the City. No one seemed to know where your family had moved to. By the time a couple of months had passed, I realized that I was pregnant. Our one night of sharing our love, had culminated in me now expecting our baby. Martin, I was terrified, what was I to do?" I interrupted her, saying, "Alexis, I wrote diligently to you every day. When I never got a response from you, I thought you had decided not to write to me." At this point, tears were forming in Alexis's eyes, when she whispered, "Did my mother intercept my letters, hiding them from me? What a wicked thing to do. Was that all I was to her, a paycheque coming into the house?" Alexis continued, "When I realized what was happening to me, I knew I had no other recourse but to speak with my boss at Caterpillar Tractor Company, to see if he could help me. I had no one else to turn to. Things evolved very quickly from there on. Mr. Salter contacted his sister in Chicago, Illinois, who agreed to sponsor me, and arrangements were made for me to immigrate to Chicago. I didn't tell anyone of my plans because, at this point, I felt you had abandoned me, and I couldn't bring shame on my family by being an unwed mother."

At this moment, Alexis put her head on her hands and sobbed silently. It was all that Martin could do not to gather her into his arms, so he laid his hand gently on her shoulder and urged her to continue with her story. Alexis went on, "It took a few weeks and Mr. Salter, my employer, helped me make all the arrangements and I gathered my few belongings and left a message for my mother advising her that I was leaving and not to try to contact me. Martin, please understand my predicament. What could I do? I felt I had no other recourse but to go. You had broken my heart, things were not good at home, I had no one to turn to and that is when I reached the decision to speak with my boss. Believe me, I was desperate. Within the space of a few weeks, all arrangements had been made and there I was, boarding a flight for Chicago."

"When I finally arrived there, Mr. Salter's sister and husband made me feel so welcome and took me into their family, organized a visit with a doctor, then helped me secure a job, then an apartment. Life was hard for me. I had no one to talk with, other than my co-workers, but I was not about to share my private life with them. So, I buckled down, made the most of it, worked hard and saved a little money, because I knew that I would not be able to work immediately after the baby was born.

Our son, Marty, came into the world and, looking into his little face, then I knew that I had to make things work for us, he would need me now, more than ever. During my visits to the hospital for check-ups, I met this young nurse, Mary Ann, who was to become a dear friend to me and, with her friendship, she helped me emotionally, especially knowing what had happened to me and how I ended up in the United States of America.

As soon as Marty reached his first birthday, my neighbour, Mrs. Mack said she would babysit if I needed to get back to work. I jumped at this chance because my meagre savings were dwindling fast. Our son was the spitting image of you…. dark hair, olive skin, and those eyes, those beautiful brown eyes that filled my heart with love for him, more so because he reminded me of my one and only true love, you Martin. I never stopped loving you, even though I thought that you had abandoned me. I knew, deep in my heart, something must have happened. I knew the kind of person you were, and it was unfathomable that you would desert me. I did return to work, and Mrs. Mack took care of our son. He thrived, as all young babies do, and before too long, I had saved enough for a little car and my world revolved around Marty and my job and that seemed to suffice.

The years passed quickly, and one day, one of my co-workers, Josh, asked me if I would go out with him for dinner. I was reluctant, but he convinced me it was just as a friend. This became a weekly occurrence and during that time, he explained that he was aware that I was a single mother and was raising my son alone. He then suggested we could come to an arrangement whereby he could help me raise him. Call me gullible, but we did see each other occasionally and, in my naiveté, was convinced he was sincere. Well, we had a quiet wedding ceremony, all too soon, things started to change. He became sullen, morose, was drinking heavily and I noticed my son, Marty, was becoming withdrawn. Too late, my husband's behaviour was a deterrent to my son. To make a long story short, Martin, I realized my mistake, how was I to alleviate this predicament? I decided to give my husband an ultimatum, either shape up or ship out, as I was not about to jeopardize my son's happiness, not for him, nor anyone. He saw that I was determined and did try to keep his drinking under control. I also spoke with Marty, who was wise beyond his years, about the conversation I held with my husband." Marty smiled and said, "Mom, I will believe it when I see it."

Throughout his childhood and adolescent years, there was always friction between Josh and Marty, and the drinking always escalated the situation." Martin remained silent during Alexis's explanation and, although he held his tongue, his heart was aching for both Alexis and Marty, for all the anguish and heartache they both had endured, but, he remained silent, urging Alexis to continue with her story.

Alexis looked into Martin's eyes and saw the compassion, giving her the courage to continue. The love of her life was sitting across from her, not judging, but listening, but she had to continue, he had to know how and why she made the decisions she had carried out. If he could find a fraction of the need she carried for him in her heart, then all would be well. She realised he had to be told all the facts of what had happened. Taking a deep breath, Alexis continued, "Martin, giving Josh that ultimatum made me more resolute than ever. My son was my priority and Josh knew it. As time went by, he slipped and, as usual, apologising it would never happen again. Then, I was spared more heartache because God intervened and Josh's health deteriorated quickly, caused by the excessive drinking, then one night, he passed away in his sleep.

Marty, by this time, had graduated from university with great marks, and he earned many scholarships, which alleviated the necessity of paying University tuition. His goal was to become a Veterinarian and, luckily for him, one of the scholarships came from a prestigious university in California. Now, he was going out into the world and I could carry on working.

One day, shortly before departing for his new venture, I had been cleaning out some of the closets in the house, when I came across a jewellery box, which I purchased shortly after arriving in Chicago those many years ago. Sitting on the bed, I opened the box to find some old brooches I had gathered over the years and, tucked away in the corner of the velvet-lined box, there was a square pad of cotton wool. I picked it up, not remembering what it held, then upon unwrapping it, there sparkling in the morning sunlight was the Topaz Butterfly. I gasped, clutching the pin to my heart, and the tears started flowing. Unbeknownst to me, Marty had come into the room quietly, because he could not hear me moving about and he was concerned. Seeing me crying, he gathered me into his arms, asking me what was wrong. My resolve melted and I started to tell him about his real father, you Martin. He was mesmerized as my story unfolded. I told him about the ritual of the Topaz Butterfly which was given to the oldest son of his forefathers, who then would give it to his wife as a token of his love for her, and so on.

It was such a relief telling him the story that I had kept hidden over the years, but he was curious as to why I had never pursued looking for you, Martin. To be honest, I guess I was afraid to find out the truth that you probably had decided to end the relationship. I also had severed all ties with my family, so what purpose would I have to start searching for you?

While attending University, Marty met Melanie, who was modelling to pay her University tuition. When they both graduated, he asked

Melanie to marry him and he gave her the Topaz Butterfly. That was when her friend Joanna had taken some photos of her wearing the brooch and that is where we are at now."

Alexis sat waiting to see my reaction. I stood up from the table and walked to the window, quietly reflecting on what had taken place. What was I going to do? I knew that all the feelings of love that I had for Alexis had been buried over the years, yet, here she was, in the flesh, telling me her story which, to me, was plausible. I was now at the crossroads of letting my heart rule my head. My mind was now made up. This was Fate giving us a chance to rectify all the wrongs that had befallen them. I slowly turned to my one and only love, holding out my arms, where Alexis rushed into them, holding on to me for dear life, as I whispered in her ear, "Darling, I would now like to meet our son." As I hugged Alexis to my chest, I felt my heart beating wildly, as though it was ready to burst open, now that I had been told I had a son. My mind could hardly comprehend how my life was turned upside down within the last couple of days. After all these years, my first and only true love, Alexis, had come back into my life. Holding her close, I looked into her tear-stained eyes, kissed her passionately, then whispered in her ear, "No more tears, we have found love once more." Alexis then quietly said, "Martin, as I have told you, our son has been made aware who is real father is, although he is not aware that I have found him. Especially, when you arrived at the hotel and then left abruptly, without being introduced to him. I will go back to the hotel and fill in all the blanks with him and make a time and place for our meeting. It should only take a day and I will call you on the phone. Darling, if he is as happy as I am, there will be no problems. Marty and I have always had a strong, loving relationship and I know that, above all, he wants me to find happiness." At that, we hugged once more and agreed to contact each other by phone the following day.

As last, our dreams were coming true, love had returned into our life. It is funny how things turn out. For over 25 years, the love of my life had dominated my thoughts, thinking what could have been. When I thought to myself, "would have, could have, should have, was now a reality." Here I was, just returning from being face to face with Alexis and all of those wonderful memories of her came flooding back. She had aged really well, although those fine lines around her eyes told me that her life was fraught with bad memories. There were a million questions running through my brain, wanting to know how life had treated her, but there was plenty of time for that. It was evident that Alexis still had feelings for me, but there was a reticence about her, I sensed her body language was one of doubt, not sure of how to react to me. After all, I had unexpectedly appeared into her life after 25 years, then having to tell me I was the father of her son, our son. I knew, of course, all of this could be straightened out with time. Our next step was for our son, Marty, to meet me.

When Alexis opened the door to her hotel room, Marty and Melanie rushed over to her anxious to find out where she had been and what had we spoken about. Sitting on edge of the bed, she slipped out of her coat, before carefully laying it over the chair, positioned at the foot of the bed. She reached out for Marty's hand and, grasping it, blurted out, "Sweetheart, finally I have come face to face with your father. It is a long story, but suffice to say, he is overjoyed at the news he has a son and he is so anxious to meet you." No sooner had the words come out of her mouth, when she saw his face light up with a beautiful smile, as he said, "Mom, I have waited all my life to hear those words. You have told me, throughout my life, bits and pieces of your life and how your love for who my real father was. Deep down, I hoped that one day your wish would come true and that both of us would have the last piece of the puzzle to complete your hopes and dreams." He could see the tears of happiness glistening from her eyes, as her heart was overflowing with joy hearing Marty's comments. She felt that the meeting between father and son would soon be coming to fruition, just the way she had hoped and envisioned it would be. She then told Marty that a time and place was to be made, whereby they could arrange to meet up with Martin. But, in the meantime, her excitement made her forget that she had not eaten anything since breakfast and now was as hungry as a horse. She arranged for room service, while discussing the plans for the next day.

Meanwhile I must have fallen asleep on the bed and was awakened by the phone ringing. It was Alexis, whose voice was brimming with joy, advising me that both she, Marty and Melanie would meet me for lunch at my Hotel at noon. She also alluded to the fact that Marty was over the moon at the prospect of meeting me. That eased the butterflies in my stomach, as I did not quite know what I was going to say, or do, when meeting him.

Promptly at noon, I was sitting at the table where I had made the reservations for a lunch for four and, as I was glancing at the menu, I heard my name being called. I looked up, saw Alexis and just slightly behind her was this young man. I gasped....it was like looking in a mirror, here was this young stranger with dark hair, tanned skin, brown eyes and a big beautiful smile, it truly was my son, no doubt about that. I extended my hand out to him and, as we shook hands, he smiled and said "Dad, this is something that I had always hoped for and it's wonderful that we have finally met." Not being an emotional man, I could feel tears stinging behind my eyes, but I gruffly made a coughing sound and, still holding his hand in a firm grip, I said, "Marty, this has been a momentous day for me too." I glanced over at Alexis, who was blowing her nose frantically, trying to compose herself, while gripping Melanie's hand. No words were spoken for a minute or two, and then we all started talking at once. I held up my hand, in a gesture of trying to compose everyone and settle everyone down. Alexis was the first to speak, "Martin, there is so much ground to cover and so much to catch up on, but, let us order something to eat and we can make other arrangements later. I feel we will be in a better frame of mind when we have had a meal."

After the meal was over and everyone seemed so naturally comfortable with each other, I then asked Alexis if we should spend some time together during Marty's short vacation in Glasgow, to get reacquainted once again. She agreed, without any hesitation, and as I had a previous surprise for her in mind, I told her that I would pick her up from at 11 o'clock the next day.

50

Conclusion

The next morning, I arose early and, since my date with Alexis wasn't until 11 o'clock, I made a phone call to my sister and then to the shop, to put them all in the picture. I made my way to the Hotel and I was just in time to see Alexis step out from the elevator. She looked every inch a ravishing beauty. She was wearing a powder blue and white dress, which stopped just above her knees and was held up only by one strap on her right shoulder. Her necklace was also light blue and was resting just above her cleavage. The tan high heels she wore elongated her legs immensely, making her stand taller. Her lips were extra glossy today and her make was done perfectly, bringing out her natural beauty. At first glance, I wanted to grasp her in my arms and hold her so close to me, capturing the wonderful thrill of this moment. "Good morning, are you ready for your mystery tour?" "Good morning Martin, just you lead on and I'll follow," she replied. I put my arm around her waist as we left the Hotel, then ushered her into the parking lot and, as we got to my car, I couldn't resist the temptation of taking her in my arms and kissing her passionately, parting her lips with my tongue and I was rooted to the spot when she responded in kind. I could have stayed locked in her embrace, but I wanted to spend as much time as possible getting to know her once again,

As we drove along the highway, I soon found that she still had her wonderful personality. She laughed at the slightest provocation and her laughter had such a pleasant sound and we were soon chatting as though we did this every day. She asked me what I did in my spare time and if I was excited about being back in Glasgow, but while she appeared interested, she seemed more focused on me. She was so warm and sincere, and I found it so comfortable with her that I began telling her more than I had ever shared with anyone before.

As soon as we arrived at the coastal Town of Saltcoats, we made for the beach and she couldn't wait to kick off her shoes and peel off her stockings to walk barefoot along the sand. I followed suit and so we walked along the shore sharing all the different and important things that had gone on in our lives. As the waves lapped around our feet, she suddenly went quiet and I could see she was lost in thought. Perhaps she was remembering the time we spent in the caravan and our first night of lovemaking. I could see that she had regained her composure, as she asked if I ever regretted how our lives changed after that night. "Alexis, my only regret was getting on the train that took me to England away from you, It left me with an anger and emptiness that I carried throughout all the lonely years, but the moment I saw you at the Hotel, my life was once more on its axis and I liked the feeling too much to ever let it leave." The moment she heard that, she put her arms around my neck and gave me the type of kiss that you want to last forever, and that told me all I needed to know.

After a while, we stopped off at a small café and had lunch, holding hands across the table like a couple of young teenagers on their first date. As the day lengthened, we went back to the car and sat talking again about the wasted years we had lost. We were so engrossed in our reveries that we lost all track of time and it was only when the sun was slipping below the horizon, we began our journey back home.

The next few days were spent taking Alexis, Marty and Melanie to some of the local spots that attract the tourists; Loch Lomond, Stirling castle, Glasgow Cathedral. These nostalgic visits gave Alexis and me the chance to prove we still relished the love that we had once shared. It was reignited with such passion and that was when I knew I just had to return to Chicago with Alexis and Marty, to get some indication if that type of lifestyle would be amenable to me, especially now that I had a family and to find out if I could up sticks and settle there, as it was important because it could be a true life changer for me, but one thing I was sure of, I was never going to let Alexis disappear out of my life ever again.

As they were all returning home the following Saturday, we all agreed to have a meal at their Hotel on the Thursday night. I arrived at the Hotel quite early and sat in the lounge, having a drink, as I waited to see them enter the restaurant. That was my cue to join them and get seated at a table. There was a jovial atmosphere as we sat exchanging all sorts of funny occasions that we had all experienced over the years. As I sat listening to the conversations, I could not take my eyes off Alexis, watching her every movement. She still had that captivating smile and her eyes seemed to have that extra sparkle tonight. When I told them that I would drive them to the airport on Saturday, and that I would be following them to America as soon as it could possibly be arranged, I could see the delight on their faces at being told of my plan.

When it was time to leave, having said my goodnights to Marty and Melanie, I stood alone with Alexis and asked her if she would mind if I stayed with her on Friday night, as it meant we could all leave early Saturday morning to drive to the airport. "That would be wonderful, of course you can, Martin," she replied. "I'll be going out for some last minute shopping with Melanie on Friday afternoon and when I return, I'll give you a call and you can come to my room."

I spent most of Friday watching an old movie on the television, before listening to the radio as I waited for the call from Alexis. It was around 4 o'clock when she called to say she was back at the Hotel and I responded by telling her I would come to see her after 6 o'clock, giving her a chance to chill out after her shopping trip.

When I arrived at the Hotel, I headed straight for her room, longing for what I had been missing. When she opened the door, she was wearing a blue negligee which left nothing to the imagination. We both stood for a few moments as though we were seeing each other for the first time. The next thing I knew, she was in my arms kissing me into submission, as our tongues met, thrusting and dancing in unison. When I wrapped my arm around her waist, I could feel her breath quicken, as her breasts crushed against my chest. All I wanted to do was touch her everywhere and hold her as close as possible to me. I broke away from her kiss and said, "Alexis, we can't stand like this forever, why don't you show me your bedroom where we can be more comfortable." I believe she knew what was about to happen, as she took my hand and led me into her room. What caught my attention were the modern décor and the large bed that was placed close to the mirrored closet, making it possible to see yourself on the bed. "Would you care for a drink Martin, there's a small liquor cabinet, well stocked with all sorts of alcohol." "Perhaps later," I replied, and pulled her onto the bed beside me. Our oral assault began once more, kissing, biting and letting our hands roam freely over each other. She wrapped her legs around me, linking her ankles together as she opened herself to me, feeling my hardness against her, until I was thrusting my shaft inside her love tunnel. The more I pressed into her, the more uninhibited she became. I could hear the soft moans as they escaped her lips. I wanted more and grasped her tightly as she raised her hips off the bed to help me drive deeper inside. Suddenly, she arched her back and cried out "Oh God, Martin." Her body seemed to spasm and tremble and, as she dug her nails into my back, I felt her wetness ooze onto my thighs. I could not control myself any longer and my final thrust exploded, spewing my seed deep within her. No words were needed as Alexis lay her head on my chest. We were both spent and completely sated and, as I enfolded her in my arms she looked up, smiled and softly whispered, "I love you Martin Sinclair." At that, we both drifted off to sleep, ensconced in each other's arms.

We stayed in bed early Saturday morning, relaxing for a while, and then showered before going down to meet Marty and Melanie for breakfast. When we got to the restaurant, they had finished their meal, so Alexis and I had a light snack. We all sat and talked about how they had a wonderful visit and wished they had more time to stay longer. We then made sure that everyone's passports and airline tickets were in order and checked to make sure nothing was left behind.

We gathered up the luggage, placing them in the car and headed for the Airport. Once there, Marty and Melanie gave me a goodbye hug and took their luggage into the departure lounge. As Alexis and I stood holding hands, I could see she was on the verge of crying, "Hey! We don't do tears here, we're the happiest couple in the world and, in any case, you'll be seeing me as soon as I can come to America to be with you." I walked her to the departure gate and with one final kiss, watched her walk away.

Driving back home, I realised how fortunate I was to have a woman like Alexis in my life. Now my utmost desire was to be with her in America to begin our new life together, as a family.

Manufactured by Amazon.ca
Bolton, ON